Ill Wind

The Valkyrie Series
Caribbean Pirate Adventure

by

Karen Perkins

LionheART Publishing House

First published in Great Britain in 2012 by
LionheART Publishing House

This edition published 2016
Copyright © Karen Perkins 2012, 2016

LionheART Publishing House
Harrogate
UK

www.lionheartgalleries.co.uk
www.facebook.com/lionheartpublishing
publishing@lionheartgalleries.co.uk

Caribbean, 17th Century, United States, Pirates, Women
Pirates, Slavery, Sea

Cover Design by CC Morgan Creative Visuals

Author's Note

Throughout the Valkyrie Series, I have used the historical and phonetic spellings of place names, and where possible taken these from Edmund Halley's map of 1699.

The Caribbees 1683

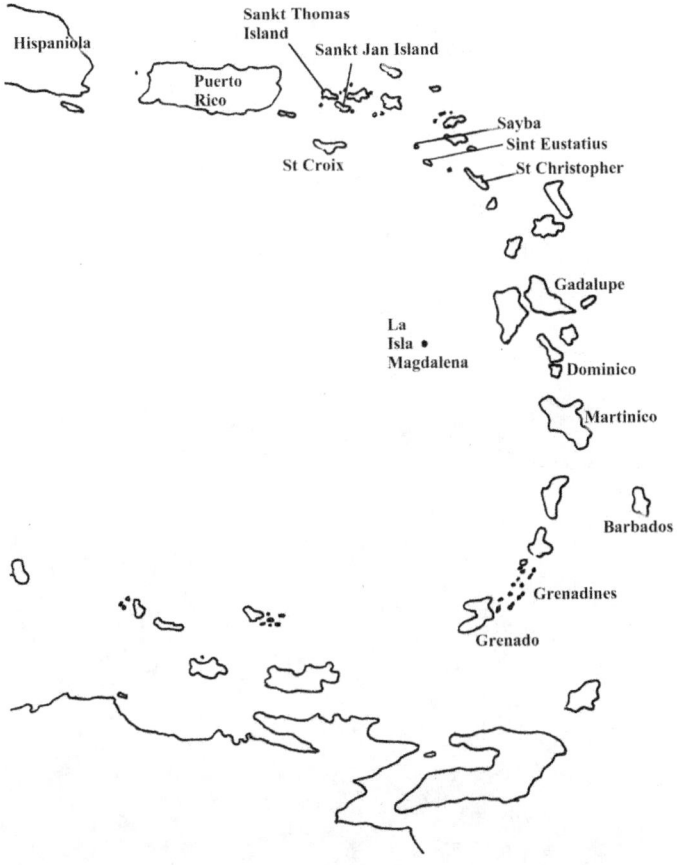

Ill Wind

Part 1

31st May 1683

Chapter 1

"What do you think he wants, Mam?"

"I don't know, Gabriella." Mam frowned at me. "Just hear him out and don't react. You know how he hates it when you answer back."

"But he's never summoned us to work before!" Father was the chief customs officer in charge of all shipping in and out of Massachusetts Bay, and was very proud of his position—nobody could trade in the colony without his consent. He usually forbade us from bothering him at the docks, although that was no hardship—the sheltered water there stank with all the waste thrown overboard from anchored ships, and turned my stomach, although it would be worse in a couple of hours when the sun warmed and rotted the putrid filth.

"Very well," I agreed.

We looked at each other, worried, and Mam reached up to tuck a wayward curl behind my ear, then gave me a nervous smile.

"Elizabeth!" Father called. I smiled back at Mam; everybody but Father called her Ellie.

"About time. I want you to meet Mijnheer van Ecken." He presented the tall, distinguished-looking gentleman standing by his side. Father hadn't looked at me yet, but this stranger hadn't taken his eyes off me since our arrival.

I looked back at him. He didn't smile; neither did I.

"And this—" Father said with a flourish, "is my beloved daughter, Gabriella."

I jerked my eyes away from the stranger and stared at Father in shock. He'd never described me as beloved before, never mind introduced me as such. I glanced at Mam; her normally rosy cheeks had turned pale. I tried to swallow, but my mouth was dry. *What's happening here?*

"She'll do." The stranger, Mr. van Ecken, spoke for the first time, and my eyes darted back to him. He still didn't smile.

"John?" Mam asked, warily.

"Great news, Elizabeth, I've procured for our beloved daughter—" that word again "—a most suitable match. Mijnheer van Ecken here is one of the West Indies' most successful merchants, and his son, Erik, is looking for a bride."

Mam gasped and turned paler still. I just stood there. Had Father said bride?

"You must remember my mentioning Mijnheer van Ecken," Father continued, oblivious to our reactions. "He's one of my best customers." He laughed, slapping Mr. van Ecken on the shoulder. The man attempted a smile, but it failed.

"He has done us a great service by selecting Gabriella as his son's bride, and this is the start of a very lucrative partnership between our families."

I looked at him and cringed at the delight on his face. I knew I should say something, but nothing came to mind. *Bride? West Indies? Married?* But I was to marry Peter! We'd been talking about it for ages, Father knew that. My breath hitched in my throat and I pressed my hand to my chest, trying to stop the panting—all of a sudden I found it hard to catch any air. He couldn't do this. He would *not*.

"John, no—" Mam tried.

"Elizabeth!" Father reprimanded, and Mam said nothing more, just stared at the ground. We both knew he didn't like to be contradicted, especially in public. Our arguments would have to wait until we were in private, and I shuddered at the thought of the scene to come.

"Mijnheer van Ecken has been more than generous and Gabriella will want for nothing in her new home in Sayba. She should be pleased."

New home? Sayba? Where on earth is Sayba? I looked at Mam, stepping back in my panic, but she stared at the ground, too used to doing Father's bidding.

"Stay where you are, Gabriella, it's all agreed, so calm yourself and do as you're told. You're flushed, you know that makes you ugly—all those freckles! You will marry Erik van Ecken and be a good wife to him—be ready to sail on the tide."

That's three hours away. I looked at his eyes. Dark and wrinkled from working outdoors, there was no emotion there. He'd sold me to a stranger, was packing me off to God knew where, and he felt nothing.

"John!" Mam exclaimed, her shock overriding her fear. "You can't, it's too soon, she's only fourteen!"

"Elizabeth!" Father thundered, his square jaw set, and I knew it was only the stranger's presence that stayed his fist. "I've made my decision." He glared at her, and her shoulders slumped in resignation. I gritted my teeth in frustration. *Why can't she stand up to him? Why can't she stand up for me?*

Tears rolled down my face—of anger, frustration, despair. I wondered when they would stop.

Chapter 2

Mam had been incapable of words since Father had silenced her at the docks. I looked at her in frustration; she was my mam, she should be standing up for me, not breaking down like this and allowing Father to do what he wanted with me.

I'd packed my few belongings myself, breaking off frequently to comfort her, but had finally finished.

"What's going to happen to me?" I whispered.

She shook her head. "Just do as your husband instructs and make the best life you can—it's all you can do."

"Maybe I should run away."

"Oh, Gabriella, where would you go? What would you do? A worse life awaits you if you flee. You have to do as your father instructs!" She opened her arms and I fell into her embrace. She stroked my hair and I knew I'd have a devil of a job to tame my wild, dark curls back into some sort of order. I shrugged. *What do I care about that, now?*

A knock at the door jolted us apart. I opened it to one of Father's wharfmen.

"It's time," he said.

I nodded at him. He sounded upset as well. He came in, picked up my small chest, and we followed him. Mam was still crying. My own tears had dried. I couldn't believe I had to leave her and all I knew, to live with a stranger as his wife. I still didn't know what that would entail.

We walked through the Massachusetts Bay Colony in silence. I wanted to run, but heeded Mam's warning. There was nothing outside the colony, just wilderness with all its dangers—unless I ran to the sea, and I could see no way of doing that.

Past the meeting house, the small wooden cottages of our neighbors, fields full of crops, woodlots and pasture. My heart leapt when I saw Peter. We'd known each other since we were babes and were best friends, but Mam's hand on my arm stayed me and I could only stare until I'd left him behind.

"Gabriella." Mam stopped and grabbed my arm. Words failed her again and, sobbing, she stretched her arms behind her neck and unfastened her necklace. I'd never known her take it off before.

"Your father gave me this—your true father," she said, "the earl." Mam had been a housemaid he'd taken a fancy to, then shipped off to the New World when she—or rather her belly—had become too much trouble. She'd met John Berryngton on the passage out.

She fastened the necklace around my neck and I looked down at the purple teardrop of amethyst, then held it up to the light. My own tears started to fall again and Mam hugged me.

"Get a move on! The tide won't wait for you!" We sprang apart at Father's words and Mam kissed me, then we continued our walk toward the docks—toward my future. I watched Father stride ahead and felt a glimmer of hope. My future could only be an improvement on my past.

He was there, my soon-to-be father-in-law; looking at his pocket watch, clearly impatient. He stooped slightly and wore a gray curled periwig over a face full of angles—nose, cheekbones, jaw. His clothes were of good quality, although of a cut that was unfamiliar, just like his accent—

Dutch I assumed from his name, but nobody had bothered to confirm it.

"About time," he snapped. "The tide's about to turn, we need to on it be."

"Yes, yes, she's ready," Father said. "Take her chest to that longboat," he added to the wharfman. I watched him obey, though he avoided my eyes as he took everything I could call my own away from my home. I knew I'd have to follow. I turned to Mam and hugged her. I had no words, and joined her in sobs.

"Gabriella!" Father pulled me away. "It's time to go. Don't embarrass me, the van Eckens are important merchants. Don't forget you're representing this family! Now go."

"No!" I tried to wrench myself free of him. "I won't and you can't—" His slap made me stumble before I'd finished my protest and I huddled on the ground, shocked. I raised my hand to my stinging cheek, but he grabbed my arm again and hauled me to my feet, then pushed me toward the boat.

"Goodbye, Gabriella," Mam managed through her sobs. "Keep well and safe."

I ignored her. Even now she wouldn't fight for me. I turned at Mr. van Ecken's hand on my other arm, and allowed him to lead me to the boat. *What else can I do?*

I looked out at the bay and the ships anchored there. *Which one will take me away?* I turned. "Mam!" I cried, and almost fell when Mr. van Ecken pulled me into the boat.

By the time we'd left the wharf, I'd calmed. Mam and Father were still visible on the quayside, but they were small now—far away. I was sure Mam was still crying, and shuddered. Father hated tears; Mam would not have a pleasant afternoon, or evening.

I watched Father grab her arm and pull her away, dragging her back to the house like a naughty child. I sighed and twisted on my seat to look ahead.

I looked up at the bulk of the ship we'd approached. I'd never been aboard one before but had spent hours watching them arrive and leave Massachusetts Bay, dreaming I was sailing away in one of them. My wish was about to come true. I'd just never imagined these circumstances. *What will become of me?*

The boat bumped alongside the larger vessel and a rope was thrown down to us. I stood up.

"Not yet, stay where you are, I'll tell you when to stand," Mr. van Ecken snapped. I sat back down. I had no fight left in me.

"Now, come here and on this sit," he said a few moments later. I looked at him in surprise at his strange English, but supposed I'd get used to it.

A wooden plank, held by rope at either end, had been lowered to us. I looked at the basic seat, then at the hull, and pointed at the battens nailed onto the side like a ladder. "I'd rather use those," I said.

"You'll do as you're told! Your father told me you obedient were, though I have not much evidence of that seen. Be warned—I do not tolerate disrespect."

I looked at him in dislike, but I didn't want to go back to Father, whatever that might mean for my future. I sat on the wooden seat and allowed myself to be hauled up the side.

A thin bald man with the most startling black eyebrows I'd ever seen offered me a hand to step onto the deck.

"Greetings, Mistress Berryngton," he said, kissing my hand. "Welcome aboard *Freyja*, I'm Captain Edward Hornigold."

"Enough of that, Hornigold, get this tub moving, I don't time to waste have."

Captain Hornigold nodded and smiled at me before walking away, shouting. His men scurried around the decks.

"This way," van Ecken barked at me, and I followed him to a hole in the deck and below. I clambered down the ladder and kept following him—I think toward the back of the boat. I was nervous, my belly twisting. *What does he expect of me? Am I really to marry his son, or was that a ruse?*

Light flooded over us when he opened a door, and he stood aside for me. I walked into a cabin—a bank of windows in the back wall provided the light. There was a bunk, table and chair, my chest, and an African woman.

"This is Klara. She's yours to do with as you will. Here." He gave me a small silver-handled whip. "You might need this to remind her of that, though." He turned and left. I looked at the woman in shock, but she kept her eyes on the floor.

"Hello," I said tentatively. No reaction. A shudder made me step to one side as the floor moved beneath my feet, and I braced myself against the wall. We were off.

Chapter 3

I looked at the whip in my hand. It was heavy; heavy enough for the foot-long handle to have been forged from solid silver. It was decorated with images of horses, but this was no horsewhip. It had three leather lashes, each about three feet long and knotted at the ends. The last few inches were darker than the rest, and I realized they were stained with blood. I threw it onto the table and looked back at Klara. Her eyes darted to the floor. She'd been studying me as I'd studied the whip. I stepped closer to her and tried again, "Hello Klara, I'm Gabriella."

She raised her eyes to mine, but said nothing, and I stepped back again under the force of her glare.

"Um, could you help me unpack, please?"

Again she said nothing, but turned to my chest and started pulling out the few gowns I possessed.

I lay awake on the small cot whilst Klara lay on a mat on the floor. I couldn't possibly sleep. On the one hand, I *was* sailing away from Father, *and* his stinking harbor, but I was also leaving Mam and Peter behind and had no idea what I was sailing toward—my future was blank in my mind. I wondered if I'd ever see Mam again. I missed her already, missed Peter, and missed having a friendly face smiling at me. I was terrified of the woman who lay on the floor, knowing she hated me.

I turned onto my side to study her in the gloom. I couldn't see her well but pictured her slim yet full body; wild black curls escaping from her headscarf; full mouth and nose. I'd heard about the dark-skinned people from Africa, but had never seen one before today. The way people talked, I'd thought they were ugly and dull-witted, little more than beasts, but this woman was beautiful. Intelligence shone out of her eyes in the way she glanced at me, full of appraisal and cunning when she thought I wasn't looking. I caught a flicker of movement as those eyes opened and I rolled over; for some reason ashamed to have been caught watching her. I vowed never to underestimate her.

I was startled by a knock at the door.

"Just a moment," I called, flustered. *Who could be asking for entry to my cabin at this time of night?*

Klara rose and lit a lantern, and I pulled on my robe. She waited for my nod, then unlocked and opened the door. A young sailor stood there, probably in his early twenties— maybe a couple of years older than Klara. He was very handsome—or would have been had he been cleaner. I could smell him from across the cabin.

"I beg your pardon, Mistress Berryngton," he said with a French accent. "I am Cheval, *Freyja's* quartermaster. The captain sends 'is apologies, but 'e would like to see your slave in 'is cabin."

"Very well," I said, confused. *What does the captain want with Klara?* But it was none of my business.

Klara shot a hate-filled glare at me, then followed the sailor out of my cabin to the one next door. I sat back on the cot in relief once the door had closed behind them, glad to finally have a bit of time to myself. I realized I couldn't remember my selected husband's name, and tears began to roll once again. "Oh Mam," I whispered to the empty room. "What's going to happen to me?"

*

My sobs quietened, and I realized I could hear more cries. It must be Klara—as far as I knew, we were the only women aboard the ship. A man cried out as well, though in pleasure, and I finally understood why Klara had been summoned. And I had given my consent. I raised my hands to my mouth in shock; no wonder she hated me. Now I'd proved myself deserving of her contempt.

I covered my ears as the screams and grunts rose in volume and my sobs restarted. I wasn't sure whether I cried for Klara or myself. Presumably Mr. van Ecken condoned this. *What will my life be like as his daughter-in-law?*

I didn't sleep that night, and lay alone in the dark until dawn slowly lightened the cabin. The door opened and Klara entered.

"Are you all right?" I asked.

She nodded, but didn't speak and limped to her sleeping mat.

"Your eye!" I exclaimed. It was bruised and half-closed. She gave me her hate look again, but now I didn't blame her. She lay down and curled into a ball with her back to me.

"I'm sorry," I whispered. "I didn't know." Nothing. Once again, no reaction. I stared at the ceiling. *Will my husband do that to me?*

Chapter 4

I was thrown against the cabin wall hard enough to wake me, and lay on the cot for a few moments trying to work out where I was and what was happening.

Oh yes: aboard a ship; sold into marriage to a stranger; shut inside a cabin with a woman who hates me.

Everything moved far more than it had yesterday and the ship was rocking violently from side to side, which is what had woken me so rudely. There was more noise, too: the sea as we crashed through it; thumping from overhead; as well as the creaking of wood and cracking of sail. I was thrown against the wall again and grabbed the edge of the cot, then looked up. *Where's Klara?*

I pulled myself to sit on the edge of the bed. She wasn't in the cabin. Fresh salty wind, a relief after the stinking air of the harbor, blew my curls over my face and I realized the door to the ledge outside was open and Klara was leaning over the rail. I jumped up and staggered toward her, bracing my hands against the ceiling to stop myself falling.

I reached the balcony door and clung to the frame. The sea had changed from a beautiful calm blue to a forbidding dark gray, and I shivered.

"Klara!" I called.

She looked up at me, then leaned over the rail again and

retched. I sighed in relief; she was seasick, not trying to jump, although I didn't understand why she was ill now. The fresh air had quietened my own stomach.

"Are you well? Can I help you?"

She shook her head. "Leave me," she said.

I hesitated. They were the first words she'd spoken to me, but I didn't want to leave her alone in such misery.

She retched again. "Leave me!" she repeated, more insistently.

I went back into the cabin. She'd been humiliated enough in the day I'd known her: once when van Ecken had given me the whip, and again by Captain Hornigold. I would not humiliate her further.

I crossed to the jug and bowl on the table and poured out a small amount of water to wash myself. I noticed the table had a wooden rim built into it to prevent the china falling, but I'd poured out too much and water sloshed everywhere. I washed my face as best I could considering I needed one hand to hold on, then turned to find something to wear.

Klara had laid out an emerald-green gown, which went well with my dark hair and pale complexion. I stripped my nightgown off and pulled a clean shift over my head. It wasn't easy with one hand and a moving floor. I picked up my stays and looked in the glass, wondering how I would tie them, when they were taken from me.

Klara wrapped the garment around my middle and I adjusted it so the wooden supports were as close to comfortable as possible. She pulled on the strings and I gasped in pain. She loosened them slightly and I thanked her; she nodded. Progress. We finished my dressing in silence and I sat down. I noticed the whip had gone from the table and didn't care—I hoped she'd thrown it overboard.

A loud explosion startled both of us, and we looked at

each other in horror. We could see nothing but sea behind, were we being attacked?

"I'm going to find out what's happening," I said to her with a bravery I didn't feel.

"No!" She bowed her head, then added, quieter. "You'd be better off staying here, out of their way."

"I need to know what's happening, and if Mr. van Ecken or the crew don't have the courtesy to inform us, I'll have to go and ask them." I couldn't stay blind in the cabin; I had to know.

I stumbled to the door, unlocked it, and went out. What had yesterday been a dark, quiet deck was now filled with light and men. Holes in the side had been opened, and I now saw the deck was full of guns; each with its muzzle pointing out through one of the gunports. I didn't like this, but I couldn't slink back to the cabin and Klara after my show of bravado.

There were posts at intervals supporting the ceiling, and I made my way from one to the next; managing not to fall until I reached the ladder van Ecken had led me down yesterday. I climbed up, kicking my petticoats out of the way to find every foothold.

Up on deck, wind whipped at my face and body, and I stumbled to the empty rail to hold on. The rail on the other side was full of men shouting and making an awful noise, and I saw another, bigger, ship a few yards away.

Musket fire sounded above me and I looked up. Men were in the rigging and crowded small platforms up there, firing at the ship, and a blood-red flag streamed above them.

I gasped, I knew what that meant—pirates! Father had put me aboard a ship of pirates!

I screamed when my arm was grabbed, and van Ecken shoved his face in mine. "What are you doing? Get back to your cabin; this is no place for my son's wife!"

"But, but, but . . ." was all I managed. It didn't seem worthwhile to point out that I hadn't met his son, never mind married him.

He pulled me roughly back to the hatch in the deck.

"But, what's happening?" I managed.

"Business," he said. "Just business." He stood over me as I scrambled back down the ladder and followed me to the cabin.

"These men were hired by your King Charles as privateers. Now the wars are over, what are they supposed to do? You can't blame them for continuing a trade in which they excelled, and I'll that ship and her cargo have for a very good price—business."

He pulled open the door and shoved me inside. "Now stay there until I give you leave to go on deck!"

His words were accompanied by a tremendous boom. I fell as the ship lurched over and the gundeck and cabin filled with acrid, stinking smoke. He slammed the door. I crawled to the cot and pulled myself onto it, tears streaming down my face yet again.

Klara sat in the far corner, as far away from the door and rest of the ship as possible, clutching her knees, terrified.

"Pirates," I told her. "They're pirates."

She nodded, put her head on her knees, and hugged herself.

Chapter 5

Things quietened maybe half an hour after I'd found out the truth about my hosts, but that half hour had been the most terrifying of my life.

We'd sat and listened to gunshots and screams; fallen when our ship bumped into the other; coughed when the cabin flooded with gunsmoke; and stayed together silent and unmoving when the other hull cut out most of our light. We could do nothing but pray for it to be over.

Now that it was, I didn't know what to say or do. I went to the privy ledge outside, but didn't use it as I'd be in full view of the other ship now sailing along to one side and just behind us.

A knock at the door startled me, and I came back into the cabin as Klara opened it. Three men stood there. Two held plates of meat and beakers of rum punch—our dinner—and Klara took the plates from them. The third I hadn't met before. He was clean-shaven and dressed differently to the others—oh, he had on shirt and breeches, as did the rest of the crew, but he also wore leather boots, a frockcoat and sported a neat curled periwig. He looked almost respectable, although the way his eyes flicked over my bodice was anything but.

"Good evening, Mistress Berryngton." He bowed. "I'm Henry Sharpe."

"Good evening," I replied. "Where's the other one, Cheval?"

He looked a little taken aback, but recovered without any loss of manners. "He's taken the helm of our prize, sailing alongside." My jaw clenched at the casual way he talked about the other ship. "Mijnheer van Ecken is also aboard and has charged me with your care. If you need anything, please don't hesitate to ask."

I nodded, his manners shaming me into remembering my own. "Thank you, Mr. Sharpe," I managed. "Um, there is one thing." I paused, embarrassed, but had to ask. "Is it possible to have a chamber pot? I cannot use the privy ledge with that ship so close."

He smiled but didn't laugh. "Of course, I will see to it for you. Forgive me, I should have thought about that."

I smiled, still embarrassed, and the pirates took their leave. I crossed to the table where Klara had arranged the food, and sighed. Every meal so far had been the same: meat, meat and more meat; although this time we had a treat—an onion. Raw and whole, but still, something other than meat. I supposed the sailors ate like this every day. I picked mine up and bit into it, enjoying the sharp taste flooding my mouth.

"What meat is it this time?" I asked Klara.

She took a bite and smiled. "Goat," she replied.

"Goat?" I asked. I hadn't eaten goat before. "What's it like?"

"Try it," she urged. "It's delicious, watch out for the bones though, their cook is no butcher." She pulled a sliver of bone from her mouth to demonstrate.

I sat and picked up my knife, stabbing a slice of meat. Dark-yellow fat was already congealing on the plate and my stomach turned, but I was hungry. I put the meat in my mouth and chewed. Klara was right, it was full of flavor, and I stabbed another piece.

I sat back, replete, my plate empty, and watched Klara clear the table. She'd definitely grown a little friendlier after the events of the day, but not much.

I took a sip of rum punch and someone knocked on the door again: Henry Sharpe holding a bucket, which Klara took without a word, then handed him the plates. He passed them to another man behind him then cleared his throat. "Ah, my apologies once more, Mistress Berryngton, but the Captain, ah, would like to see Klara immediately."

I heard Klara's gasp and my shoulders stiffened.

"My own apologies, Mr. Sharpe, but I require Klara's services myself this evening. I regret I am unable to comply with Captain Hornigold's request." My voice sounded firm enough, but inside I felt liquid.

He gave a small smile and nodded. "Very well." He left.

I let my breath out in a sigh—I hadn't realized I'd been holding it—then slumped against the wall and looked at Klara, who was staring back at me.

"Can you pass me that bucket, please?" I'd been holding it in all day, and really needed to relieve myself, especially after that.

"Th . . . thank you," Klara stuttered as she passed it to me.

"If I'd known last night—" I couldn't continue, but she understood, nodded, and turned her back as I used the bucket. When I'd finished, she took it and threw the contents over the rail of the privy ledge.

Another knock at the door; this one heavy and insistent. Klara and I looked at each other, then I shook my head and opened the door myself. The captain stood there, his face red with anger, and I couldn't take my eyes off his black bushy eyebrows. He looked at me, then over my shoulder at Klara, then back to me. I noticed Sharpe standing behind him.

"What's the meaning of this?" he asked, his voice loud.

"I beg your pardon?" I asked, pretending confusion.

"I have requested Klara's company this evening."

"I beg your pardon," I said again, "but I require Klara's services myself this evening."

"Why?"

I stepped back, for some reason I hadn't expected to be challenged. I thought quickly and held onto the door; my legs felt weak and I wasn't completely sure they could hold me up on their own. "I need her to prepare my bath."

"Bath?" This is a working ship, not a traveling inn," the captain said, his voice full of scorn.

"I am aware of that, Captain, but I'm on my way to meet my future husband and I'd like to bathe." I knew I had to stay calm, but it was an effort.

"I could cut down one of the hogsheads for her," Sharpe said from behind Hornigold. "That may work as a bathtub." Hornigold turned and glared at him, and I was interested to see him take a breath to calm himself. Sharpe was unaffected by his anger.

"You sort it then," Hornigold snapped. "And get one of the deckhands to fetch warm water from the galley." He turned back to me, calm now. "It's all organized, my crew will arrange your bath, Klara is not needed."

"I'm not having any of your filthy crew in my cabin!" I retorted. "They can leave the buckets of water outside the door, and Klara will take it from there. I'll also need her to help with my dressing. I cannot possibly spare her at all tonight." I looked him in the eye and refused to blink or let my gaze drift up to those eyebrows. I noticed Sharpe wink at me from behind him and felt myself blush, but I didn't back down.

"Klara is *my* slave, and is here to attend to *me*," I continued. "I am sure my fiancé will be very interested to hear *all* the details of my journey."

Hornigold clenched his fists and made a noise like a growl, then spun round and strode away. Sharpe smiled at me and followed. I closed the door in relief, then sighed. I was shaking and felt faint, but was cheered by the flicker of a smile from Klara. *Why couldn't I have stood up to*

Father like that? Why did Mam not resist Father like that?

My return smile dissolved into giggles that I couldn't stop, and Klara soon joined in. I'd been terrified defying the captain—a pirate—like that and had expected a blow. Who'd have guessed a villain would stay his fist where Father would not? Eventually, my relieved hysteria subsided, and I sat on the cot to wait for the bathtub and water. I had to focus on the future and not the past if I was to survive this.

"This worked tonight, but we need to find more reasons why I can't spare you," I said.

Klara looked up, then smiled and crossed to the cot. She knelt down and reached underneath it, then pulled out a chest I hadn't realized was there. I moved out of her way as she opened the lid and looked inside at lace, ribbons and a parcel of white silk.

She lifted out the silk, and said, "We have to make your wedding gown. It could be a lengthy task."

I stared at the material, feeling numb as it finally sank in that I was to marry into this life, and Mam would not be there to guide me.

Chapter 6

Mr. van Ecken summoned me, and I left Klara packing my chest and joined him and Captain Hornigold on the deck at the back of the ship above the cabin. I looked shoreward. There it was—Sayba. We'd entered a small bay, bathed in sunshine, around which a town huddled.

"Eckerstad," Mr. van Ecken said with pride. Klara had been tight-lipped about my fiancé, Erik, but she had told me about the town. Eckerstad had been founded by the man beside me—Jan van Ecken—and he was also Governor. It was the only town on the island, and Jan and Erik lived in the largest estate—my new family was the most important in Sayba.

Captain Hornigold shouted, "Let go anchor!" and a man on the foredeck swung a large mallet. The anchor, which had been suspended on a wooden frame to the side of the bow, dropped with a tremendous splash. The ship slowed and swung round until the anchor warp jerked tight and we were held in place.

"Ready the longboat!"

It was time to go and van Ecken led me to the side of the ship and that carrying seat suspended from the spars above. I didn't protest this time but sat in silence, drenched with sweat in the heat, as I was lowered to the small boat already loaded with our chests. Van Ecken then Klara followed and we were rowed ashore.

A short, heavy, red-faced man with a basic open carriage was waiting for us. *My fiancé?*

"Rensink," van Ecken gruffly greeted. "Where's my son?"
Not Erik then. I sighed in relief.

"He sends his apologies for not meeting you in person, there was an important matter that needed his attention."

"Hmpf!" Mr. van Ecken did not seem pleased. "May I present Mistress Berryngton? This is Rensink, Brisingamen's overseer," he introduced. "Erik should be here his wife to greet," he continued.

I stayed silent—I'd already learned it was the best tactic where Jan van Ecken was concerned.

We climbed aboard the carriage; van Ecken sitting up front with Rensink, who took the reins of the single horse. Klara and I sat behind and the chests were lifted up into the bed of the cart. We left with no farewells to the sailors who'd brought us here.

We were soon surrounded by jungle and I gazed about me at every shade of green imaginable and every description of bloom: red spikes, soft yellows, blues, pinks and more. The air was flooded with scent and filled with noise, and the heat made me feel faint—it could not have been more different from Massachusetts Bay.

After half an hour the trees thinned out and we drove through sugarcane fields. I noticed something to one side, and peered closer, then faced Klara to ask about it. Her head was turned and she refused to look or answer. I turned back, fascinated, until the shape of it started to make sense. A cage—just large enough to hold a man—and suspended from one of the larger trees. We drew level and I gasped when I saw the base was littered with bones.

"The slaves may have the strength of beasts, but they also have the minds of beasts." Van Ecken had turned in his seat to address me. "They need sometimes reminding who their masters are."

I stared at him in shock, unable to find any words, and he turned to face forward again.

"Here we are—Brisingamen," he said a few moments later and with obvious pride. I craned my neck to see past him and Rensink to catch my first glimpse of my new home.

It was very large: two stories painted gold, with a steep roof and a short, squat tower at either end. A broad veranda ran the length of the front and overlooked a large lawn. It made Father's cottage in Massachusetts Bay look like a shack. I smiled, although I couldn't quite shake the image of that cage from my mind.

Chapter 7

I followed Mr. van Ecken through the largest of the seven arches framing the veranda into a large entrance hall in the center of the house. Dominated by a grand staircase straight ahead and with the walls painted white so as not to clash with the black-and-white tiled floor, it was an ostentatious display of the van Eckens' wealth. I could see only two doors, one to the left, the other to my right, and I jumped when two men dressed in indigo livery with gold braiding appeared out of the shadows behind the staircase.

"Hans, Hendrik, get the chests from the carriage," van Ecken ordered. They both nodded once and gave us a wide berth as they walked outside. I smiled as they passed me, but neither met my eyes.

I glanced at Klara, but she also kept her eyes to the floor.

"In here," van Ecken said, marching to the left-hand door and opening it. I walked through into a large, airy drawing room. Decorated in gold-flock wallpaper, it had three large settees and a number of small carved tables.

A large oil painting of a formidable-looking woman dressed in black dominated the walls, and she looked across the room toward the veranda and outside. I crossed to the veranda doors and looked out at the large expanse of garden in front of the house, and wondered what there would be to do here.

Raised voices disturbed my thoughts, but I couldn't

understand what was being said. I watched two men leave the house; they looked quite similar in that they both had broad shoulders and bowed legs; just like the sailors on the ship. They also wore the same clothes—linen shirts and short, baggy breeches, but these two had added all sorts of finery to the basic outfit. Good quality leather boots on their feet, colorful sashes around their waists, and the brightest, most heavily decorated frockcoats I'd ever seen. One was in cochineal red with lace at the cuffs and collar, braiding around every hem and seam, embroidery in between, plus large brass buttons.

The other wore bright yellow over an emerald green sash with similar fripperies. They had clashing silk scarves over their heads, and large-brimmed hats on top. I'd never set eyes on such gaudy gentlemen in my life, and I giggled to myself, imagining the reactions if they walked into the puritan Massachusetts Bay Colony dressed like that.

Hans and Hendrik appeared leading a couple of horses for them, but I turned as the door to the room opened and didn't see them leave.

Mr. van Ecken entered ahead of a younger man. *Erik?* They didn't acknowledge me at first, but continued arguing in a language I didn't understand. I looked from one to the other as they quarreled, wondering what they were saying and feeling very uncomfortable.

The younger man—presumably my husband-to-be—looked presentable enough. About my height, he wore a tightly curled periwig—the yellow of which clashed with his dark, exaggerated mustaches. He'd dressed with care, his clothes of obvious quality. *Although the gold buckles on his shoes are overdoing it a bit.* I looked back at his face—his lips were thin and eyes cold. There was very little expression on that face, and I shuddered a little. He didn't look like a man who smiled very often.

"This is her," the elder van Ecken finally said in English. "Gabriella Berryngton."

I stepped forward. "Pleased to meet you."

He looked me up and down, then said something else to his father that I couldn't understand. It did not sound complimentary. He stepped toward me, bowed stiffly and took my hand to kiss.

"Welcome," he said, coldly. "I'm Erik van Ecken. The wedding is planned for next month so you have time to prepare. There'll be five extra for dinner—tell Belinda and organize the menu. I have work to do." He left the room.

I looked at the father. "Belinda?" I asked.

"You haven't met Belinda yet?" He sounded angry. "What is that bloody girl thinking?" He marched to the door and shouted for Klara. I flinched. When did he think Klara had had chance to introduce me to anyone? Why hadn't he made any introductions himself? He hadn't even introduced his son—I'd been forced to guess that was who he was.

I realized then what Erik had said. *The wedding's arranged for next month. Did they make the arrangements before finding a bride?*

My thoughts were interrupted by Klara's entrance. I noticed she gave Jan a wide berth.

"About time, girl! Your mistress hasn't been introduced to Belinda yet—see to it! She has a dinner party to plan, apparently our nautical friends are joining us." He marched out and Klara and I looked at each other in amazement.

"He doesn't seem to like these 'nautical friends'," I remarked.

"With good reason," muttered Klara. "I'll fetch Belinda," she continued before I could ask what she meant.

Chapter 8

I lay my head against the edge of the bathtub and sighed. Klara looked up from her unpacking and giggled. "You've had a bath nearly every day that I've known you. I'm surprised you don't wash away!"

"I know." I laughed with her. "I hated them at home, barely had one a month, but it was the only way I could think of to keep you out of Hornigold's cabin—there's only so much sewing I can do in a day. They must have thought me mad!" Klara stopped smiling and put her head down. "And it's so hot here, I'm going to need one every day just to cool down," I carried on, trying to rescue the mood.

Klara looked up at me again. "Thank you," she said. "He'd have carried on taking me every night if you hadn't stopped him."

"I'm sorry about that first night, I didn't understand—" I tailed off again, not knowing what to say. Klara stayed silent. I hoped I hadn't spoilt the tentative friendship growing between us.

She shut the lid of my chest, which had been placed at the foot of the ornate four-poster bed. There hadn't been much to do; I'd found a full wardrobe of gowns through a door off my room—all of them of much better quality than even my best. Mine would stay in the chest.

I looked around the room. The bed itself was draped with fine muslin curtains and smothered in velvets and brocades. The walls were also richly decorated in a deep red and hung with tapestries—even the floor was adorned with rugs—and the furniture was solid and elaborately carved. My chest looked completely out of place.

"Would you cover that with something please, Klara?"

She smiled and threw a length of burgundy brocade over it. I thanked her and thought back over the events of the day.

"Belinda seems very nice," I said, and Klara smiled and nodded.

"I don't know what I'd do without her," she said. "She arrived a couple of years ago from England with her husband, John." I leaned back with my eyes closed to listen to her story. "They'd signed up for five years servitude, but John died within weeks—of the jungle fever."

"Oh no!" I sat up, shocked at the misfortune of the large, friendly woman I'd met earlier—the only person so far who'd welcomed me on sight.

"Yes, it was the same fever that took Mevrouw van Ecken—that's her in that picture over the fireplace in the drawing room. Horrible woman she was."

I nodded, remembering the painting, and I realized there was a fireplace in this room too. *Why do we need fireplaces on an island this hot?*

"Anyway, Mijnheer Jan told her she'd have to work John's passage off as well as her own—I don't think she'll ever get away from this place."

"The poor woman," I exclaimed. "But she's so cheerful."

"Yes, she keeps saying she has nowhere else to go, and at least she's needed here."

I didn't know what to say so changed the subject. "What about these 'nautical friends' that are coming tonight—do you think Hornigold will be one of them?"

"Sure to be. And his quartermaster, Cheval, do you

remember him? There'll be Captain Tarr and *his* quartermaster as well, Blake. And probably Sharpe, too, though he's not too bad."

I stared at her in horror. On my first night in my new home, I had to dine not only with my overbearing future father-in-law and my downright rude fiancé, but near half-a-dozen pirates—one of whom at least already hated me. "How am I going to do this?" I whispered. "I can't think of anything worse."

"Oh, there'll be worse all right, believe me, there'll be worse." She spoke quietly and I looked up at her, not sure I'd heard her properly.

"We'll make sure you're dressed perfectly, so Mijnheer Erik can't find fault—I know what he likes and what he doesn't. Stay as quiet as you can at the table—don't give them reason to notice you—that would be my advice."

I nodded, unable to find words, then stood so Klara could dress me.

"Ow! What are you doing?" She'd put the stays around my middle and was pulling the strings extremely tight behind my back. The belt with the supporting wooden bars was cutting into my flesh.

"That's how he likes it, as tight as possible. It's just for the evening, you'll hardly see him during the day."

I bit my tongue and trusted her to prepare me for the ordeal ahead.

Chapter 9

I made my way downstairs and entered the drawing room through an elaborately carved door. The room was empty.

I sat down, but was too nervous about the evening ahead and uncomfortable in my new gown with the tight stays. I stood again, and wandered over to the picture of Erik's mother. She was dressed in black with a high white lace collar and stared out at the room in disapproval. *Had that been her usual expression? It must have been if she was painted that way.* Her brow was furrowed, her nose hooked and her lips almost non-existent, but that could just have been the effects of her bad humor. I peered closer at the frame: *Adelheid*—a beautiful name for an ugly woman.

I turned quickly as the door opened to men's voices. Jan, Erik and the two gaudies from earlier came in first. My heart sank as I recognized Captain Hornigold behind them, Cheval was also here—and Mr. Sharpe. Was I really to dine alone with these seven men? It would have been unheard of in Massachusetts Bay. I straightened my shoulders and held my head high—I would not show these men my unease.

"Good evening," I said.

"Goedenavond," Jan van Ecken replied, which I assumed was good evening in Dutch. Erik only grunted.

"Captain Hornigold, Cheval and Sharpe you already

know." Jan waved an arm in their direction. Hornigold and Cheval smirked, but Mr. Sharpe offered me a small bow.

"And may I Captain Tarr and Quartermaster Blake present?" The Gaudies approached me. Tarr was the one in red, Blake wore the yellow. They both bowed, kissed my hand, and murmured greetings. I concentrated my entire will on not cringing away from them.

I looked at Erik; he hadn't yet greeted me properly. He'd donned a dark green frockcoat for the evening and carried a silver-tipped cane. He looked very distinguished and I offered him a small smile. Jan barked something at him in Dutch and he walked over to me and took my hand.

"You look lovely," he said.

I dropped my eyes and blushed. Angry at the reddening in my cheeks, which I knew made my freckles even more obvious, I whispered my thanks. We were saved from any more awkwardness by the entrance of the two liveried men from earlier carrying trays of drinks. Wine for myself and the van Eckens; what smelled like rum for the sailors.

We sat with our drinks, Erik next to me on one of the sofas, and struggled to find conversation until the dining room doors were opened—our cue to walk through to the table.

Erik showed me to a chair next to his at one end of the table, his father sat at the far end, and the sailors arranged themselves in the remaining seats. I was relieved to find Mr. Sharpe sitting at my left, although was not looking forward to a meal sitting opposite Captain Hornigold.

Jan said grace and Klara, Hans and Hendrik brought in the food. Soup to start, then the stewed goat I'd agreed with Belinda earlier. I looked up at Klara as she placed a plate in front of Erik and froze. His hand was on her thigh, and she had not reacted.

I gasped in shock and was aware of Hornigold smirking

across from me. Klara wouldn't look at me and Erik didn't seem to have realized anything was amiss until Jan spoke sharply in Dutch, and he snatched his hand away.

I stared at my plate, mortified, with no idea of what to do or say, but knowing from years of living with Father not to make a scene, especially in front of company.

"So, are you enjoying being on dry land again?" Sharpe asked, his voice light and breaking the tension. I turned to him gratefully, and told him how beautiful the island and house was. I carried on talking—most of it nonsensical and my voice shrill, but he feigned interest. Soon, the rest of the party struck up conversations and the incident was over. I smiled my gratitude at Sharpe and started to eat, desperate for the evening to be over.

The meal passed in a blur. Erik hardly spoke to me, and the pirates were loud, coarse and thought nothing of swearing at the table. Only Sharpe paid me any attention, and I was aware of drinking more glasses of wine than was prudent.

I concentrated on using the knife and fork, and wondered if we would be using them every night. At home, the forks were only used when we had company, the rest of the time we used our fingers. I was amused to see Hornigold and Cheval struggle with the dainty instruments, and giggled to myself as I saw their food dropping from the tines so often that they were reduced to watching the others to see how the forks were properly used.

I excused myself as soon as I was able, leaving the men in the drawing room and escaping to my room. I pulled the cloth covering my old chest away. I didn't fit in here, but I wouldn't hide, nor would I hide my belongings.

Klara entered a few minutes later and I glared at her, the wine emboldening me.

"You said something earlier, that you know what Erik likes."

She said nothing, just looked at me, her face expressionless.

"Exactly what is your relationship with my fiancé?" I asked as mildly as I could.

"Relationship?" She laughed. "The only *relationship* is that of master and slave. I was born into slavery, and given to Erik on his sixteenth birthday. I was twelve, and he could do with me what he wished. If I didn't please him, I was beaten." She looked at the floor, tears in her eyes. I felt ashamed.

"He still does whatever he wants with me," she continued. "I dare not refuse him. His beatings have got worse since he started using that cane, and his father hates me—he would welcome any opportunity to lock me inside that cage we passed on the way here and leave me to starve or thirst to death." She looked at me again, tears running down her cheeks.

I remembered Hornigold on the boat, and how meekly Klara had gone to him that first night when she'd been summoned, and felt sick. *Is that all she knows of men? Is that all there is to know? Do I really have to marry a man such as that?*

I stood and passed her a lace kerchief to dry her eyes. I wanted to hug her, but something held me back. She dried her eyes and pocketed the kerchief.

"Would you like those stays loosening now, Miss Gabriella?"

"My goodness, yes! I could hardly eat, they're so tight!" I was relieved to move off the subject. I needed time to think about it all, my head was awhirl.

Klara's fingers started the laborious task of untying the various layers of my gown and I put my hand to my head.

"Are you well, Miss Gabriella?"

"Dizzy," I gasped. In fact I felt as if I was going to faint.

"It's because of the stays—lean forward and put your head between your knees, I'll fetch you some water."

I did as I was told, and did start to feel better. I straightened when Klara returned with a glass of water and sipped gratefully.

"Better?"

"Yes, thank you."

My head had stopped spinning and I started to relax. I wanted to ask her why Jan hated her, and why he hadn't sold her in that case, but couldn't find a tactful way of phrasing my questions. They'd have to wait for another day.

I sighed in relief as the stays were finally removed and I massaged the tender skin of my stomach, which felt bruised. Klara took a pot of something from the dresser.

"Belinda makes this—it's wonderfully soothing for damaged flesh.

I scooped out a handful and rubbed it into my belly, and Klara did the same for my back. I stared at the wall in silence.

Chapter 10

I was woken by Klara. I blinked at her for a few seconds and looked around the room; the events of yesterday, and especially the revelations of last night rushing back to me. I sat up in bed and she put a breakfast tray on my lap. I managed to mumble a thank you—a poor response considering she'd had to carry it from the cookhouse and up two flights of stairs to my room in the small turret on the right-hand side of the house. I suddenly realized somebody would have had to carry all that water the same distance for my bath the night before. I wouldn't be able to soak so often.

I sipped the lemongrass tea. A bit cold, but it tasted well—very refreshing and perfect for breakfast. The tray was laden with strange fruits, toast and preserves. I spread a thin slice of toast with the preserve, in the hope it may still be warm. It wasn't, but the jam was delicious.

"Oh, what's this?" I exclaimed.

Klara smiled. "Mammee apple. It grows wild on the island, and Belinda makes the preserve."

"It's delicious!"

I cheered up a little. I may be marrying into a family of brutes who consorted with pirates, but I was away from Father and the food was exquisite. At home, it had been bland and boring—usually porridge or stewed rabbit.

In the Caribbees I'd already found goat and mammee

apple, what else was waiting for me to discover? I looked at the fruit as I ate, enjoying the tang of the preserve, but wanting to finish it so I could try the next new flavor.

Klara busied herself about the room, pouring water into the basin, then taking and laying out another set of clothing for me to wear.

"Where does Erik sleep?" I asked her, suddenly thinking about my married life. *Will I have to leave this room or will he join me here?*

"In the room below," she answered. "And Mijnheer Jan has a room on the same floor but at the other end of the house. There are two guest rooms between them, and another in the far tower."

It was the most talkative she'd been so far, and I realized she was relieved at my friendly tone after last night's disclosures.

"And where do you sleep?"

In one of the huts beyond the trees, unless I'm . . . I'm . . . required at the house." She dropped her eyes and I pressed my lips together in disapproval. Then I realized I wasn't being fair; Klara had no choice, she wasn't to blame for the arrangements.

"Well, I'm sure you'll be spared those duties once Erik is married," I said. She glanced at me quickly and turned so I couldn't read her expression.

"Would you like the blue or the green gown this morning?"

"The blue, I think," I said, watching her pile stays, petticoats and mantua onto the bed, and wondering what she wasn't saying. I sighed and rose to dress.

"Don't pull the stays so tight, Klara! I'm still sore from wearing them like that last night!"

"But Mijnheer Erik, he likes stays to be tight, Miss Gabriella. He always says he should be able to put both hands around a woman's waist and his fingers meet."

"I don't care what *Mijnheer Erik—*" I sneered the name "—says about ladies' waists. He is not my husband yet, and he does not decide how I dress. Loosen it, Klara, it's too tight!"

She said nothing, but obediently loosened the ties.

Downstairs, there was no one about. I wandered into the drawing room, but there was nothing to do in there. I decided to explore my new home and crossed the hall to the other carved door—a nautical scene to complement the others.

I gasped at the large room full of books I'd stumbled upon. I loved to read, but at home we'd only had bibles and prayer books; this library was a dream come true. I wandered about the shelves, looking at spines, and was dismayed to find only Dutch titles. Of course, why would the van Eckens have an English library?

Disappointed, I crossed to the other door in the room and opened it.

"What the Devil do you think you're doing? Get out of this room! At once!"

"Oh!" I gasped at my welcome from my future husband. Jan was also there, but didn't speak. "I'm sorry," I stuttered, backed out, and shut the door. I ran out of the library and out of that house, across the lawns and down the road. I'd never felt so humiliated and unwanted, not even at my father's house.

I tried to keep my eyes averted from the hanging cage, but found it impossible. Despite my intention to give it as wide a berth as I could as I passed, my feet took me closer. I glanced inside and gasped. Two human skulls lay in a litter of picked-clean bones. I shuddered, had a living man been locked inside with the bones of a dead?

I ran past a field of sugarcane, turning left up a smaller

road that I hadn't spotted when I arrived, wondering what could be up there, yet dreading the answer.

The road opened up into a large space, surrounded by thatched buildings. None of them had walls, and none seemed to be in use at the moment. I turned in a circle and looked around me, then squinted. There was movement in the distance. I studied it for a moment and realized it was men working the field.

"What are you doing here?"

I whirled round and saw a scruffy man with a young boy—still a child, yet laden down with hoes and picks. I recognized Rensink—the man who had driven the cart on my arrival. He carried only a whip.

I squared my shoulders. "I'm looking around my estate. What's it to you?"

He looked me up and down, then smiled. I felt very uncomfortable. "Ah yes, the little English miss." I scowled. He approached me, hand outstretched, took mine and shook it. "I didn't expect you to be running around the mill."

I nodded, unwilling to explain myself. "What are all these buildings?"

He looked around and pointed each out. "Toolshed, mill, boiling house, cooling house, curing house. All that's needed to turn that cane into sugar. You'd best not come here once we start the harvest—too dangerous. Now if you'll excuse me, we have a lot of cane to weed and more jungle to clear, and those clumsy oafs keep blunting the hoes and snapping the picks." He stared at me until I turned and walked away. I looked back when I heard a cry and a clatter of metal. The boy had dropped his load; I'd turned just in time to see the man hit him.

"Stop! Do not hit that boy!"

Rensink laughed at me and hit the boy again, then turned his back and they walked away.

I stared after them in frustration, then walked back to the house, but didn't feel like going in yet. I crossed the lawns to a small path I could see leading into the trees. I would find out where that went.

I soon came out of the trees and halted at the sight before me. I stood on a cliff top and looked out on leagues of sparkling turquoise water. It was the most beautiful sight I'd ever seen. I looked behind me at the trees—why on earth had they screened this view from the house?

Cheered, I started to walk along the cliff top and squealed in delight when I spotted a small beach below me. There was a path too; steep and not often walked, but it *was* a path, and I scrambled down it.

On the sand, I removed my stockings and shoes, and reveled in the feel of warm sand between my toes. It was so *fine*. I walked closer to the water's edge, lifted my skirts and paddled—the water was *warm*. I squealed again when a larger wave splashed me, and made my way back to the warm sand to let the sun dry my feet and gown. Life would be far from perfect here, but there were definite compensations.

I shivered and looked at the sky. Clouds were moving in to obscure the sun. Reluctantly, I donned my footwear and started the climb up the cliff. I was getting hungry anyway, it must be near lunchtime.

I slipped once or twice, but was able to steady myself with my hands and didn't have too much difficulty. At the top, I looked down at my gown and grimaced. White salt spots around the hem showed where the sea had caught me, and there was a small tear in the left sleeve. I'd have to sneak up to my room to change and hope Klara could fix it. Next time I came here, I would wear one of the gowns I'd brought with me.

The path was hard to follow through the undergrowth and trees, but when I emerged I saw my sense of direction wasn't too far out. I was at one corner of the lawn rather than the center that I'd aimed for, but that was better; I could hug the trees and not cross the empty space in full view.

Suddenly, I was drenched. The clouds had burst in a rainstorm the likes of which I'd never seen before, and I ran toward the house, all thoughts of concealment washed away.

I clattered onto the veranda, shaking my dripping arms and gasped. The van Eckens stood on the covered terrace, watching me.

Erik looked me up and down in disgust, turned and went inside without a word.

"Those gowns are expensive, child, you need to better care take," Jan van Ecken said and followed his son. "Get changed quickly, luncheon ready is."

I followed them: embarrassed, ashamed and furious. There had not been a single inquiry about my health after such a soaking—the concern had only been for my gown.

Klara followed me upstairs and I shivered as we got rid of the ruined clothes. I dried my hair as best I could and dressed quickly in the green gown.

Klara looked in amazement at the gown I'd discarded and I shrugged. "Do you think it can be fixed?"

She smiled at me, "I'll do my best, Miss Gabriella." I thought she was going to say something else, but she must have changed her mind.

"Are you laughing?" I asked, smiling myself.

"Not at all, Miss Gabriella." She tied the new stays loosely.

*

Downstairs again, I walked through the drawing room into the dining room and sat before a full plate of food. Jan and Erik hadn't waited for me, and were already eating. We sat in silence until the peppermint tea was served. I'd barely tasted my meal, and wondered what delicious new treat I'd been too anxious to enjoy.

"My son wishes to apologize for the way he earlier to you spoke," Jan said, breaking the awkward silence. "Our study is out of bounds, we should have told you that, before you in barged."

I nodded in acknowledgement, not sure if I was receiving an apology or a reprimand.

"The drawing room is for your private use unless we guests have. You are free for the library to use, although we'd prefer you to bring books to the drawing room to read rather than in there remain."

I nodded again.

"There is a collection of books in English near the veranda doors."

Now I looked at him in interest, but he'd finished and the two men rose from the table. Erik hadn't spoken a word.

I followed them from the room and into the library. They both ignored me and went straight into the study and shut the door. I crossed to the shelves Jan had mentioned and ran my hand over the spines.

Books in English! There must be a hundred of them. I chose one about Norse mythology and opened the door to the veranda. I could hear raised voices coming from the study, but didn't care. They could shout at each other as much as they liked.

I sat in a comfortable chair at the table in front of the drawing room and began to read, soon losing myself in tales of ancient gods, Valkyries and Nordic heroes.

Chapter 11

At the dinner table again, I stared at my plate. Jan and Erik were arguing in Dutch once more. Truth be told, it was less awkward than sitting in silence, but only marginally, and I'd had enough.

"Do you have any idea how rude you're being?" I said. They stopped talking and stared at me in surprise.

"You've brought me to this house and expect me to marry into this family, yet you rarely speak to me. Now, at the dinner table, you're speaking a language I don't understand. I can't follow the conversation. I can't join in. I am not included in any way." I was near tears with the frustration of my brief stay. Jan looked shocked, Erik angry, but I couldn't hold back the words.

"I was subjected to the company of pirates at my first dinner here, and have never heard such language or seen such table manners before. I have not been shown around the house or estate, and was spoken to in the worst manner imaginable when I explored on my own!"

I stopped, breathing heavily, surprised at myself. I'd never have dared to speak to Father this way, and I could barely believe I'd found the courage to speak to the van Eckens like this. I only knew I couldn't live the rest of my life the way I'd lived the last few days.

After a moment, Jan spoke. "You are quite right, my child, we have been neglecting you. There has not for two years a woman in this house been, and we have forgotten how to behave."

I smiled at him, relieved he'd taken my outburst so well. Erik still frowned at me.

"We were those very pirates you mentioned discussing."

Erik looked at his father sharply, but Jan waved a hand at him and he said nothing.

"You see, we a dilemma have, and it's taking over everything, even your wedding, my child, and we only apologize can."

"A dilemma—about those pirates?" I asked.

"Well, yes, but it's not really your concern."

"Oh, why stop now, Vader? Why not tell her it all? You want her to make a van Ecken, don't you?" I noticed his English was better than his father's.

Jan looked at his son, then turned back to me.

"Excuse my son's manners, he finds this wedding very sudden, as I'm sure you do, but this family a new generation needs." He glared at Erik again, then turned back to me.

"It's right that you should our family history know—your sons will one day need to know it.

"The van Eckens have been directors of the Dutch West Indies Company since the start, and I and my wife in 1650 came to the Caribbees. It was clear to me there would myriad opportunities in the New World be, and I wanted advantage of them to take.

"Originally based in Sint Eustatius, I moved in 1655 to Sayba once the war was over, founded the town Eckerstad, and this house built. All went well for many years—our businesses grew and the island flourished. Erik was born and we could not have happier been."

I glanced at Erik as he took a long drink of wine. He kept his eyes on his plate and said nothing.

"Five years later, Thomas Morgan—Henry Morgan's uncle, have you of him heard?"

I nodded, who hadn't heard of Henry Morgan, the flamboyant buccaneer turned knight? Even in Massachusetts Bay, he was famous.

"Well, Thomas Morgan was from the same cloth cut, and he Sayba attacked. We were merchants, not warriors, and did not a chance have. We were into servitude taken whilst strangers in our beautiful home lived."

I gasped, it sounded horrible.

"Adelheid—my wife—Erik and I were taken to Henry Morgan to serve. He had Elizabeth just married and was a sugar plantation in Jamaica establishing. It wasn't long before I running it for him was."

I nodded, not knowing what to say and having to concentrate to understand his English.

"After a couple of years, I had a good business in his name built up, and then England and the Netherlands signed the Treaty of Breda and the second war between our nations over was.

"I implored Morgan to allow my family and me to Sayba return. He had first-hand my talents as a businessman seen, and I was able to convince him that I on his sugar plantation wasted was. I could make him more money if I were able to my own empire build with him as a partner. He would a percentage of the profits take—a large percentage, I may add," he glanced at his son, "and he agreed."

"He would have been a fool not to, and Henry Morgan is no fool," Erik said.

"Quite. He did a little more than expected though, and provided me with a ship and, er, crew as well as helping me the sugar plantation here set up. Tarr was a young man then, and would goods and prize ships me bring which I would from them purchase."

"At very low prices," Erik butted in.

"Yes, at lower prices than the norm." Jan nodded slowly.

"And we would the goods on sell and fit the ships out as Africa slavers."

"Our profits soared," Erik added.

"Yes, and a large part of our profit was loaded into Tarr's hold, Jamaica bound," Jan snapped. "But for all my complaints," his voice softened, "our lives had monumentally improved. I was my own master again, we freely in our own home lived, and ran the island more or less as we before had." He paused. "We were happy for many years, until in '81 Adelheid died."

"I'm sorry," I murmured, fascinated by the story and not knowing what else to say.

"Jungle fever. Couldn't be helped. We manage as best we can without her, but Brisingamen has long enough without a mistress been." He smiled at me and I smiled back.

"But now, Governor Lynch has suspended Morgan, he is out of favor, and my father wants to break the arrangement that has served us well for many years," Erik said.

Jan looked at him in annoyance. "Henry Morgan has for nearly twenty years a millstone around my neck been. His influence and power is weak. This is our opportunity to free of him be!"

"Henry Morgan's resourceful, Vader, you know that as well as I. He may be today weak, but he will tomorrow strong again be. Tarr and Hornigold's efforts more than make up for the percentage he takes, and the island safe is." Erik's English had deteriorated with his anger. "The whole of the Caribbees know of them and they know Sayba under Tarr's protection is. No one will dare to attack our island whilst they interests here have. Keeping them close will prevent history repeating itself, and I'm surprised you can't see that!"

"With last year's profits we can our own protectors hire, preferably Dutch—Sayba would still be safe!"

Erik shook his head. "You would start another war, Vader. Neither Morgan nor Tarr would easily give up on this arrangement, it's far too profitable for them. If we set ships against them, we would lose more to sinkings than we to the Englanders give. The arrangement works, Vader. Tarr and the others are good men, and by now they are near as loyal to us as they are to Morgan. You would be a fool to now change things."

I gasped as Jan's face turned bright red at his son's insult. He glanced at me, then controlled himself with visible effort. I was gratified to see Erik look concerned— he knew he'd gone too far.

Klara and the two men brought the next course, roasted suckling pig, and we ate in silence.

Jan placed his cutlery on his plate and looked at me. "So, are you excited about your wedding, child?"

I smiled nervously. *Is he serious?*

"You only have three weeks left to wait, then you will husband and wife be!"

Erik scowled and I stared at them both. *Three weeks!* I kept my gaze on my future husband, wondering if I might shame him into a smile, but he didn't look at me. Jan spoke to him in Dutch.

"Mr. van Ecken! I thought we'd agreed to speak English at the table," I said, not sure where I'd found the courage to speak to him in this manner again. He bowed his head.

"Quite right, child, but you can't keep calling me Mr. van Ecken. Call me Schoonvader—it means father-in-law, and will soon true enough be. And don't mind my son's bad manners. He sees the necessity of the marriage, and is only with nerves suffering. All will be well once the nuptials over are." He glanced at Erik, who nodded, once.

"You must some thought to your wardrobe give, child. I understand you and that slave," he glanced at Erik again, "did some good work on the journey on your wedding gown. It needs to finished be. If you need fabric for more gowns, please let me know—we have warehouses full of the stuff, but please take better care than you this morning did."

I stared at my empty plate and mumbled an apology.

"Very well, then. I think we're here finished. You may to the drawing room retire, Gabriella. Erik and I will to the library go to continue our discussions."

Later that night, I lay in bed, my head swimming with all that I'd seen and heard that day. I was much happier, and only wished that Erik and his father would reach some agreement soon. I was still wary of my future husband, but hoped he would prove to be friendlier once this current disagreement was at an end.

I caught my breath at a sound and listened hard. It came again from below. I realized I'd heard something similar—aboard Hornigold's ship on the first night. I stared at the canopy over the bed—angry, jealous and ashamed. *If he thinks so little of me that he would bed my slave in my hearing, why on earth had he agreed to marry me?*

Part 2

30th June 1683

Chapter 12

I took a deep breath and held the looking glass up to my face. Eyes darkened with kohl, lips reddened with cochineal, face powdered with chalk, and cheeks rouged with cerise. My shining dark hair was set off well by my veil and hung in perfect curls just past my shoulders.

My gown of white silk left my shoulders bare, its sleeves were tied with more silk and fell to my elbows. The bodice was ruffled and the mantua, hanging in perfect drapes to enhance the length of my body, was embroidered with red and yellow flowers, and drawn back over my hips to show off matching petticoats. I twisted slightly to look at my back. The sash at my hips was tied into a perfect bustle and the dress trailed behind. I had never looked so well and smiled at myself. It was the last day of June—my wedding day.

"You look beautiful, Miss Gabriella," Klara said and smiled. I smiled back, but my smile faltered with nerves for the day and life ahead of me. An image of Peter floated in my mind, but I pushed it away. I could not think of him—ever again.

"It's time," she added.

I sighed and nodded, pulled on my matching gloves and picked up my fan. I was ready and couldn't put this off any longer.

*

The past three weeks had been awful. Jan and Erik had rowed constantly behind library and study door. Presumably it was still about Morgan and his pirates, but I couldn't be sure. I could only hope they weren't arguing about me. At least Jan tried to be polite and remember his manners, but Erik barely spoke to me. It was clear this marriage was Jan's idea and Erik a reluctant participant. At least we only saw each other at mealtimes and most of the days were my own.

That didn't mean much; there was only so much time I could spend sitting on a beach, reading or working at my embroidery, and my only friend was a slave who was regularly bedded by my almost-husband, whether she wanted to be or not. Looking at her now, and the genuine smile on her face, I thought I believed her when she said she did not.

I shuddered, thinking of the man I was to marry. *What kind of man would behave as he does?* I didn't want to marry him, but knew I would. I had no choice. My father had sold me to the van Eckens. I was at their mercy and had no power of my own. If somehow I found a way to leave and went home, Father would be furious. I had no doubt he would send me straight back, if not worse—I suspected he may even be capable of murder if defied so publicly.

I couldn't escape anyway. I was trapped on an island—surrounded by water. I didn't have a boat or know how to sail one. Every visiting ship worked for or with Jan and Erik, and there was nowhere else to go but jungle—full of strange sounds in the dark. I wouldn't survive a week in the Caribbean wilds—the thought of that terrified me more than the thought of life as Mevrouw van Ecken.

"Ready?" Klara's prompt shook me out of my thoughts. I nodded and moved to the door. Klara gathered and lifted my train, and we struggled down the stairs. My embroidered white silk shoes were higher than I was used to, and the excessive amount of silk I wore made the narrow, steep staircase difficult to negotiate. I breathed a sigh of relief when we reached the landing without mishap, and we walked to the top of the main staircase in silence.

This staircase had been built to make an impression on everyone who entered the house and would be much easier to descend. I straightened my shoulders and lifted my chin, determined at least to get through the day with dignity. Joy wasn't an option.

Erik was nowhere to be seen; only Jan waited for me in the large, grand hall.

"Why the hell are you that dress wearing? That one's for tomorrow!"

I looked at him in confusion. This was my wedding dress and this my wedding day.

"We arrange today the legal affairs. We only the marriage celebrate once it has consummated been—tomorrow! Well, it's now too late to change. You'll just have to it wear. Don't damage or wrinkle it—it needs tomorrow to be perfect!"

I nodded, near tears. I'd assumed the wedding customs would be those I knew, and realized now that assumption had been foolish. Nothing about these men was what I knew: not their manners, habits or language.

Jan walked ahead to the carriage. I heard him mutter, "*Vrouen,*" under his breath and cringed. By now, I knew what that meant: *women.* My slow, awkward climb into the carriage only increased his impatience, and he left Klara and Hendrik to find a way to fold my dress with a minimum of wrinkles.

Eventually we were ready and started the drive to Eckerstad.

"Is that why Mam and Father aren't here yet? Are they coming tomorrow for the celebrations?" I asked. I needed to know; they hadn't been mentioned, but I hoped with all my heart that I'd see Mam again.

Jan looked at me and sighed. "They're not coming, child. Your father is too busy and he would not permit your mother unaccompanied to travel."

"Oh," I said, stung. I blinked back tears and stared, unseeing, at the trees and scenery we passed, and clasped Mam's amethyst in my hand. How could I have been so stupid as to think they'd come?

Chapter 13

"Where's the church?"

"There is no church, child. It costs time and money to a church build. And what for? We can talk to God in the comfort of our own homes. I'm not for a minister paying to tell everyone what to think. I'll myself do that!" Jan laughed.

I tried to smile. I'd enjoyed the informal prayer time on Sundays that seemed to be the only way the van Eckens celebrated their religion. They'd been a relief after the solemn day-long worship at home, but I'd expected something more for my wedding.

In Massachusetts, life, and even celebration, was taken so seriously, a wedding was a simple statement sworn by bride and groom, at home, before a magistrate. I'd been envious of the stories I'd heard of other cultures and their big wedding services and subsequent parties, and had hoped for something like that now. But there was no one else here.

I took Hendrik's hand so he could help me down from the carriage and offered a nervous smile to Klara, who jumped down from the seat behind me and organized the dress, preventing any part of the train touching the dirt of the square. I squinted at her; her eyes looked wet, but she turned her head away and I said nothing.

We climbed the steps to the largest brick building in

Eckerstad, my arm on Jan's, Klara following, and entered the town hall. I took a deep breath and tried to calm my nerves.

Jan led me to a door on the right and opened it. He stopped, standing still a moment to look at Erik sitting behind a large, ornate desk. He said something unfriendly in Dutch and Erik rose, then walked around the desk and stood before it. Father and son stared at each other a moment, then Erik looked at me. His eyes softened and he smiled. I smiled back. *Maybe this won't be too bad, after all.*

We walked toward my almost-husband, and Jan dropped my arm to move behind the desk and take his seat. Klara arranged my dress, gave me a discreet pat on the arm, and retreated to the back of the room. I looked at Erik, then at Jan in expectation. I was ready.

Jan cleared his throat and spoke—in Dutch. My face fell. Not only was my Mam missing from my wedding, but so was my language.

Erik spoke. I couldn't understand a word.

Jan told me to say, "Ja'. I did.

Fifteen minutes later, Erik walked me back out of the room and to the square. As we walked into the bright sunshine, a loud cheer greeted us. I blinked. The square was full of people wishing us well. I smiled and offered a small wave before I was ushered into the carriage.

Jan and Erik shook a few hands and exchanged brief words with people, but I wasn't introduced. I supposed it was obvious who I was, but I'd have liked to know who was who.

With no other option I waited as patiently as I could until they both climbed into the carriage and we started for home. I stiffened with the realization that I'd thought of Brisingamen as home for the first time.

*

Jan had insisted I change out of the gown before dinner, and that Klara ensure not one speck of dirt or wrinkle remained on it by morning.

I smiled at her once we were alone in the safety of my room.

"Which gown would you like to wear to dinner, Mevrouw van Ecken?" she asked and I shuddered.

"The pale-gold silk, I think, Klara. And please keep calling me Miss Gabriella—I may be married to a Dutchman, but I'm not ready for Mevrouw yet." I laughed and she smiled at me.

I sat down heavily as the realization sank in. I was no longer Gabriella Berryngton, I *was* Mevrouw Gabriella van Ecken. I thought of Peter again, then forced his image from my mind. It was useless to think of him, I'd never see him again.

I stayed in my room as long as I could, but when I heard a door slam downstairs, I knew I couldn't put it off any longer. I rose, took a deep breath, and made my way downstairs.

The evening meal was awkward and silent. I was nervous about the night ahead. Erik barely looked at me, never mind spoke, and Jan soon gave up his attempts at conversation. It was still over far too quickly, and as we rose from the table, I thought I'd throw up what little I had managed to eat.

The men went to their study, as usual, and I stayed in the drawing room and tried to read, but could not concentrate. I had no idea what to expect from the marriage bed except grunts and screams. I was unclear about what caused them, though. My departure from Massachusetts Bay had been so sudden, and Mam so upset, we'd not spoken about my marital duties—we hadn't expected my marriage to Peter for many years. I only had advice to do as my husband instructed, and the memory of guilty gossip from my friends, and I was terrified.

I rang for Hendrik and asked him for another glass of wine "to steady my nerves", as Father used to say.

Chapter 14

I put down my empty wine goblet and book, and stood. I couldn't put it off any longer. My head spun and I grimaced. I'd drunk too much wine. It was time to go to bed.

I went upstairs carefully. I'd heard no voices when I passed the library door, but knew the heavy door hadn't been opened whilst I had sat alone in the drawing room. They were still in there: my husband and father-in-law. I giggled. *My husband.* Then hushed. *Husband. I have a husband.* I carried on upstairs.

I sat at my dresser and pulled the round enameled brush through my hair until Klara entered. She offered me a smile, but I was too nervous. I had no idea what Erik would expect of me. I wanted to ask Klara, but knew I wouldn't. I was the mistress of the house and she my slave; I couldn't ask her how to bed my husband.

She untied and unlaced until she'd removed all the pieces of my gown. She poured out some water and I washed my face, under my arms and—after a suggestive glance from Klara—between my legs.

I dressed again in my night shift—it hung to my knees, had pink ribbon decorating the neck line and sleeves, plus embroidery on the chest. Klara held up the looking glass and I stared. My face was turning brown from the sun and my freckles had doubled, at least. I looked like a child, not a married woman.

"Thank you, Klara," I said, my voice betraying my nerves and fear. She looked as if she wanted to say something, but thought better of it, put the glass away and, with a final, concerned look in my direction, left the room.

I climbed into bed, smoothed the covers over myself and lay with my head propped on a bolster. I waited.

The door banged open and I woke with a start. The room was dark, but my husband held a lantern which he placed on my dresser. I could see him outlined by the light as he undressed. When he pushed his breeches down, I looked away, embarrassed, but curiosity got the better of me and I turned my eyes back to him.

I'd never seen a man without breeches before, although knew what they had down there. As a child, I and my friends had giggled at the boys when we splashed in the sea—naked so as not to spoil our clothes. Father would have flogged us had he known. None of those boys had anything like this, though. They'd been small and floppy, I'd never expected anything so . . . aggressive, and I shrank back against the bed. I didn't want him coming anywhere near me with that thing.

He pulled the muslin tester to one side and climbed onto the bed, flung the covers back and knelt over me. I felt deeply embarrassed when he pushed my shift up, exposing me and staring in the dim light. I tried to cover myself, but he batted my hands away.

He leaned over me, bracing his weight on his hands, and looked at my eyes for the first time. I screwed my nose up at the smell of sour rum, but forced myself to stare back and tried to tell him through my look to be gentle. I couldn't read anything in his eyes, and was sure he hadn't understood.

I screamed as a pain tore through me from between my legs. Erik smiled and pushed into me harder. I bit my lip to keep my screams in. He'd enjoyed the first one, I wouldn't give him any more.

He kept pushing, over and over, until finally he groaned and moved off me. I stared at his back and was relieved when he immediately started to snore.

Is that it? As his wife, do I really have to let him do that to me whenever he wants?

I turned over onto my side, hugged my knees to my belly and let the tears come. I moved one hand to my mouth to quieten my sobs when they threatened to burst out of me. I didn't want to wake him.

Chapter 15

I woke alone in the morning. The memories of the day and night before came back to me, and I couldn't stop the tears.

I turned away when Klara entered, but by the pause in her step I realized she knew I was crying and didn't know what to do about it. She put the armful of linen she carried onto the chest and left the room again.

By the time she came back, I had myself under control, my face dry. "Good morning, Klara," I said, my voice steady.

"Morning, Miss Gabriella. Are you well?" I nodded and flung the covers back, then stood. I gasped when I saw the sheets. He'd made me bleed! He must have known, but he hadn't cared!

"Don't worry, Miss Gabriella, it's normal the first time."

I looked at Klara as she threw the covers back down to hide the red stains. "I'll take care of it." She nodded toward the pile of linen she'd brought to my room. I swallowed and nodded.

"Thank you," I tried to say, but it came out as a whisper.

I crossed to the bowl of water she prepared and winced as I pulled my shift over my head. My body hurt. I washed carefully, then dressed in the pale-blue gown Klara had laid out whilst I was washing.

"Where's the wedding gown? Am I not wearing that today?" I asked.

"Later, this afternoon," Klara replied. "You'll need to

change after lunch, before the guests arrive, but this morning is your own."

I let out a sigh of relief. After the surprises of yesterday, I didn't know what to expect from today, but at least I had a few hours as Gabriella before I had to play the part of Mevrouw van Ecken again.

At the breakfast table, Jan was all smiles and full of congratulations, and I knew I was blushing as I carefully sat down.

"Good morning," I said to my husband, refusing to allow him to ignore me.

"Morgen," he muttered, then lifted his eyes and smiled at me. I dropped my own eyes, unable to hold his gaze with that expression on his face. There was no warmth or emotion in that smile—it was a simple stretching of his lips.

I stared at my plate and picked at the fruit, my appetite gone.

"Eat up, child. With any luck, you'll be eating for two soon, you need to build up your strength," Jan said.

I froze. I couldn't imagine bearing them a child. I couldn't imagine having Erik as the father of my child. I started at a discreet touch from Klara and glanced at her. She smiled. I wondered what she was trying to tell me.

Eventually, breakfast over, I could escape. I needed to get away from the house and everything van Ecken, and headed through the trees to the cliff top, then my beach. I didn't move until the position of the sun told me it was noon.

Lunch was just as awkward as breakfast, but the fresh air had made me hungry and I wolfed down the spiced chicken. I'd barely finished when Erik sent me upstairs to change. I climbed the stairs slowly. I wasn't looking forward to spending the afternoon and evening in the company of Jan, Erik and their friends.

Chapter 16

Klara had the white dress looking perfect again, and I congratulated her as she entered my room. She nodded at my words and held out a cup of steaming liquid.

"I saw your face, Miss Gabriella, when Mijnheer Jan talked about children."

I looked at her, remembering the way she'd smiled and touched my shoulder. "I cannot bring a baby into this house, Klara. I won't let those two men raise my child, but what can I do?"

"Drink this," she said, and I took the cup. "It's a tea made from plants that grow nearby. I and some of the other women drink it every morning. None of us have had a child since."

I smiled at her, hardly daring to believe it. "You're sure? I won't have his baby if I keep drinking this?"

"I'm sure," Klara said. I drank it, and grimaced—it was bitter.

"You'll get used to the taste," Klara said, smiling.

"Or you could add sugar," I said, laughing with the relief I felt.

"Or I could add sugar," Klara repeated, smiling. "Turn around."

I did, and she untied the discreet ribbons holding my mantua in place, then removed it. Petticoats and stays followed, and I quickly washed then dressed in my wedding gown.

There was a knock at the door and we glanced at each other.

"Just a moment," I called, but the door was flung open despite my words.

"You need to hurry up," Erik said. "You've wasted the morning, you were nowhere to be seen when you should have been making preparations. Now our guests are arriving and you are still nowhere to be seen. This is not behavior I expect from my wife and the mistress of Brisingamen." He accented his words with a regular thumping of his cane on the floor and I noticed Klara flinch every time he brought it down.

"Oh, I thought everything was already done," I replied. "I didn't know I was needed—if you'd told me, I'd have stayed at the house." I noticed Klara's fingers stilled on the ties of my bodice at my words.

Erik just looked at me.

"Pull those stays tighter, Klara," he said, without taking his eyes from me. I stared back at him. I wouldn't give him the satisfaction of protesting and gritted my teeth as the wooden slats were drawn into my flesh.

Klara draped the mantua around me and secured it, and I checked my hair and face in the mirror. I was ready.

Erik turned and strode out of the room and I followed. I glanced at Klara as I left and she gave my hand a little squeeze, then I was on my own. I followed my husband down the first flight of creaking stairs, my stays digging into me on every step, but I was aware of Erik standing at the bottom watching me and I wouldn't give him the pleasure of a whimper or complaint. I glanced at the door nearest my stairs—Erik's room. I knew now we'd keep separate rooms and he would visit me at his own convenience. I wasn't welcome in his room—not that I could ever imagine myself wanting to visit him. I realized that I was effectively trapped. I wouldn't be able to descend these wooden stairs without alerting anyone in that room of my movements.

"Hurry up, wife, our guests are waiting!" Erik tapped my back in impatience with his cane and I glared at him, then swept past him toward the main staircase. He caught up with me at the top and grabbed my arm, linking it with his own. I knew it wasn't for my benefit, but for that of the crowd of people gathered in the hall and cheering.

I stretched my lips in a smile and stared at all the faces. I'd wished for a large party for my wedding day, and here it was. I knew nobody. Not one person was there for me. My eyes continued to sweep the room as we descended the stairs, and my smile became genuine when I recognized someone—Mr. Sharpe, standing with the Gaudies, Hornigold and Cheval. There was only one friendly face in this crowd of people, and he was a pirate. My smile faded.

Chapter 17

Erik led me around the room on his arm as he greeted our guests and introduced me. At least, I think that's what he was doing—he spoke only in Dutch, but when he said my name, he and the others looked at me and bowed. I gave a smile and small curtsey back. If he told me their names, I was unable to pick them out from the stream of Dutch.

I couldn't understand anyone here, so I watched them instead, trying to spot clues to the conversation in the way they held their bodies, crossed their arms or touched my husband. Also in the way they spoke—I couldn't understand the words, but I could still hear the fear, the dislike, the flattery, and I found it fascinating. I realized I'd been doing exactly this since I'd arrived to try and understand the van Eckens when they didn't have the manners to speak English in front of me.

There were few women here, and all those present were on the arm of a husband—we seemed as much a rarity in the Caribbees as the Massachusetts Bay Colony—and I smiled at every woman I met, hoping to find a friend. The only smiles I received back were of pity or embarrassment, and I began to despair. Was *anybody* here happy for us or wishing us well for the future?

I looked around me for Klara—at least she'd have a genuine smile for me, but she was surrounded by the sailors.

Eventually we, or rather Erik, had greeted each guest and we re-joined Jan. Both van Eckens ignored me and, aware of everyone in the room staring at me and their lack of manners, I was grateful when Mr. Sharpe approached.

"You look beautiful, Mrs. van Ecken," he said, and his eyes dropped to admire my dress.

"Thank you, Mr. Sharpe," I replied and stared hard. His eyes had not yet risen from my cleavage.

"Mr. Sharpe?" I said, and his eyes darted up to mine. His suddenly pale face flushed.

"Oh, I do beg your pardon, Mrs. van Ecken." His gaze dropped then rose again. "Forgive me, but your amethyst—it's such a beautiful stone." His hand moved toward it and I grabbed the pendant myself, cupping the stone in my hand to protect it from the pirate. His hand dropped.

"Where did you get it?"

I frowned at his rudeness, but decided to answer—up to now, he'd behaved well toward me and—after Klara—was the closest thing I had to a friend in the Caribbees.

"My mother gave it to me when I left Massachusetts to get married—it had been given to her by my true father."

"Your true father?"

Yes. Some English earl who persuaded her he loved her, then put her aboard a ship to the New World rather than face the consequences of his courtship. He gave her the stone as a keepsake." I wrinkled my nose in disgust.

"You don't think well of him."

"Of course not! At best he's a coward, at worst a devil. He lied to her, made her love him, used her, then shipped her off."

"What happened to her?"

"A man on the ship took pity on her and married her. But he turned out to be another devil—just of a different ilk." I looked at him, my eyes narrowed. He was asking a lot of questions. I realized my hand had dropped from the necklace as I had been talking, and he was staring at it again.

"Sharpe! Stop bothering my wife!"

My heart sank, Erik had noticed our conversation. Sharpe struggled to tear his eyes away from my chest, and Erik thumped the floor with his cane in anger, silencing the room.

"Captain Tarr!" Tarr was already crossing the room to join us. "Your nephew is drunk and making a nuisance of himself, kindly remove him from the presence of my wife. And teach him some manners!"

Tarr nodded once. "I beg your pardon, Mijnheer van Ecken, he is not feeling himself." He took one of Sharpe's arms and indicated to Blake to take the other. They half-pulled Sharpe out of the hall and into the Caribbean afternoon sunshine.

"Do not ever let me see you encouraging that man again," Erik hissed. "You are my wife and you will behave accordingly!"

He turned and left me standing alone in a sea of people. I looked around the room, embarrassed, self-conscious and confused.

I spotted Hornigold and Cheval in one corner, unable to conceal their amusement at the turn of events; Cheval even raised his glass to me. Jan stared, disapproval etched onto his features, and nobody else met my eye. Gazes darted away wherever I looked.

"Be careful, Miss Gabriella," Klara spoke softly at my shoulder. "It seems you have an admirer. Mijnheer Erik won't like that—be very careful around him."

I looked at her and nodded at the concern I saw in her eyes, then took another glass of wine from the tray she held.

Chapter 18

The rest of the wedding celebrations passed in a blur of strange faces and not-understood language. I didn't feel much different as a married woman than I had as a girl—apart from Erik's nocturnal visits, and those I could do without.

The household woke later on a Sunday and had a relaxed breakfast, then the three of us gathered in the library for prayers. As soon as I could escape, I found Klara and told her to come with me.

"But where are we going, Miss Gabriella?"

"You'll see, Klara, I want to show you something."

"But I have much work to do," she protested.

"The work can wait—you toil too hard as it is, I want us to have some fun today!" I grabbed her arm and pulled her through the trees to the cliff top.

"Isn't it beautiful?" I asked Klara. She nodded.

"Wouldn't it be wonderful if we could sail away one day, just go?"

"Go where?"

"Anywhere we wanted," I said.

"It'll get better, Miss Gabriella, just give it time, you've only been married a week."

I looked at Klara and gave her a small smile. I didn't believe her, but appreciated her trying to cheer me. We stared out to sea a little longer, dreaming of the impossible, then I urged her along the cliff path to the beach.

Once on the sand, I kicked off my shoes, lifted my petticoats, and ran to the water, splashing in the shallows. "Come on, Klara!" I laughed, urging her to follow me. She shook her head, but with a smile, and followed me to the water's edge. She took off her shoes and jumped back as a small wave covered her toes.

I laughed at her. You act like you've never seen the sea before!"

She shrugged. "Not this close."

"But how?" I was flabbergasted. "This is such a small island, and we live so close."

She shrugged again. "I don't have time. I work at the house every day, and when there is some time on a Sunday, I have much to do at my hut."

I gasped. "Oh, Klara, I didn't think. When you said you had a lot to do, I thought you meant at the house. Is Sunday your day off?"

She laughed. "I don't have days off, but there's usually a little time to clean my hut, wash my clothes . . ." she tailed off, staring at the sand.

"I'm sorry, I didn't realize. Go if you want to," I said, embarrassed at my selfishness, my assumption that she'd be happy to come to the beach with me.

"Soon," she said. She looked up at me with a smile. "I quite like this, the work can wait just a little while."

I laughed and kicked water at her. She squealed and ran back to dry sand. I followed and sat next to her, laughing.

"Mama! Mama!"

Startled, I looked round at the voice and saw a small boy scrambling down the cliff path. I squinted and realized I'd seen him before, at the sugar mill.

"Who's that?"

"My son," Klara replied, without looking at me. She got up and went to meet the boy.

He was small, maybe four or five years old, and was much lighter skinned than Klara—not much darker than myself now that I'd spent a month or so in the Caribbean sun.

They spoke for a while, then the boy ran off, looking round at me before he started to climb.

Klara re-joined me on the sand. "He and Wilbert were worried, they couldn't find me at the house."

"Wilbert?" I asked.

"He's one of the field slaves—he was there at the wedding celebration."

I remembered the dozen or so men dressed in the same livery Hans and Hendrik usually wore, and carrying trays of drinks and food.

"I didn't know you had a son," I said, shocked at how little I knew about this woman who was my main companion. "What's his name?"

She glanced at me, then looked back out to sea. "Jan."

"I beg your pardon?" She had spoken quietly and I thought I'd misheard.

She looked me in the eye. "Jan," she repeated, louder this time.

I stared at her, the implication of the name hitting me. I felt sick. "Jan," I repeated. "Oh, Klara." The revulsion I'd felt at first was swept aside by pity.

Klara looked out to sea again. "You know I was given to Mijnheer Erik for his sixteenth birthday—put into a pretty dress with a ribbon tied in my hair." She snorted with something like laughter. "My mama was so proud that I'd be working in the big house, and when I didn't come home at night, she thought I had a nice room of my own. She wouldn't listen to anyone who told her different."

"Not even when you told her?"

"I couldn't tell her what was happening, what Mijnheer Erik wanted from me every night. Her heart was already weak, all I could do for her was give her the fantasy."

"But, but, you said you were twelve?"

She nodded. "It didn't matter to Mijnheer Erik—I was just a slave girl to do with as he wished—my age didn't matter."

"And you had a son."

"Yes, I had a son—I didn't know about the tea then. Mijnheer Erik left me alone when my belly started to grow—and his father ignored me. In fact, I think he was pleased—they would have a free slave!"

I turned away, unable to look at the expression on her face. "But why did you call him Jan? You were forced! Surely calling him Jan celebrated his father?"

She laughed; a desperate sound with no humor in it. "I was young. I thought by calling him Jan they would recognize him as blood—show him favor, maybe even free him."

"They didn't," I guessed.

She made the laughing noise again. "No, they didn't. They put him to work as soon as he turned four. He's been weeding and picking up sugarcane after the harvest for two years already. Wilbert does his best to keep an eye on him, but he comes home covered in injuries.

I thought back to the boy I'd seen. I could hardly believe he was six years old—he certainly didn't look strong enough to do a day's work.

"He's stronger than he looks," Klara said. "He needs to be."

I looked at her in sympathy.

"Mijnheer Jan hates him; hates that I named him for him. If it weren't for Mijnheer Erik, I'm sure he'd have killed us both a long time ago."

"What? Why?"

"If you name someone for a Dutchman, you give the child a piece of their soul."

"What?" I didn't understand.

"Mijnheer Jan believes that by naming my son Jan, I have stolen part of his soul and given it to the boy." She looked at me. "He wants it back."

I felt cold and shivered. I remembered the way my father-in-law had been with Klara on the ship, and the way he'd spoken to her since.

"And Erik is protecting you?" I asked.

She nodded. "For the moment, at least. But now you're here, I don't know what to expect. I had hoped they'd both mellow with a new mistress of the house, but—" She paused and stared at the waves.

"At least he gave me to you when you came. Mijnheer Jan can't dispose of us if we're not his. But if Mijnheer Erik grows tired of us—" she paused again and I noticed tears running down her face. She turned to me.

"If you have a child, he *will* tire of Jan, and my son will die."

"Oh, Klara." I thought of the little boy who had scrambled down the cliff path to his mama, and tears ran from my own eyes. I didn't want Erik's child, not at the moment, anyway. But what if that changed? I may want a child one day, but if Klara was telling the truth—and I did believe her—then the birth of my child could mean the death of hers.

Chapter 19

I'd been going to the beach every day. It was the place where I found it easiest to think, and a place I was never disturbed. I had been cool toward Klara since her confession, though knew I wasn't being fair. She was a slave and had been given from one man to another, used and violated, then vilified for the consequences. She'd been even younger than I was now when it had started. I shuddered, my heart going out to her and the poor, frightened child she'd been.

I reached the cliff top and stopped, shading my eyes from the sun. Yes, I knew I'd seen something—a ship, its sails glinting in the harsh sun. As I watched, some of the sails were taken in—she must be coming to the island.

I walked along the cliff, watching the ship draw closer to shore. *Surely she must tack soon?* If she carried on much further, she wouldn't be able to clear the headland between here and Eckerstad. But she kept coming.

The beach was below me, but I didn't climb down. I sat instead and watched the ship sail closer to the rocks, my heart in my mouth. She was going to wreck.

I knew I should run and get help—those men would soon need it—but my legs were jelly. I couldn't stand, I could only watch. Closer and closer. I wanted to close my eyes, but needed to see.

I gasped—she was through! She kept coming and jarred

as she ran aground. I stood, my legs strong again, to get a better view. Her remaining sails were dropped and an impossible number of men ran about her decks and climbed down to the beach.

As the crowd on deck thinned, I recognized bright flashes of color—the Gaudies. Captain Tarr and Quartermaster Blake were here.

I stared for a moment at the invasion of my special place, then turned and walked slowly back to Brisingamen. Belinda would need to know there may be extra mouths to feed this evening.

I went through my usual routine: deep breath, shoulders back, head up, then opened the door—and stopped in surprise.

The drawing room was full of people. The Gaudies were here, as expected, but also *Freyja's* men—Hornigold, Cheval and Sharpe—and there was a woman with them, too. I stared at her, wondering who she was. She was beautiful: long, dark hair tumbled down her back, pale skin—despite the sun—contrasted with her dark eyes, but she didn't smile.

Hornigold stepped back for a moment, and she came fully into my view. Her gown was simple and of quality, though she must have been wearing it for a number of days and it was starting to look tatty. I wondered what had brought her to this house, in this company, and we gazed at each other: two lost souls.

Hendrik opened the dining room door. I wouldn't have chance to speak to her yet—maybe at the table.

But no, she was seated as far away as possible from me on the opposite side and at Jan's left hand. Sharpe took the seat next to her, and I was surprised to feel a pang of regret. Of everyone at this table, he was the one man whose conversation and company I enjoyed.

Cheval took the seat to my left, and smiled at me. I offered a polite smile back. With his square jaw and pale-blue eyes, he was a good-looking man, but I always felt uncomfortable in his presence. His eyes were cold, and his face portrayed little expression, whatever his topic of conversation—which was usually himself. I never knew what he was thinking, but couldn't shake the impression that it was often contrary to what he was saying. I picked up my knife to spread butter on bread.

"Mevrouw van Ecken." I looked up at Sharpe. "Forgive me, I was unable to introduce my companion to you beforehand." I smiled at him and the woman. "This is Magdalena Ortega. Magdalena, I'm honored to introduce Gabriella van Ecken."

We smiled and nodded to each other. Erik grunted and I looked at him, wary of his mood.

"My apologies, Mijnheer van Ecken, Magdalena was . . . an unexpected guest. I didn't feel able to leave her aboard ship with the crew."

I noticed Hornigold glare at him and realized there was something more going on here.

"She should not be with you at all!" Erik finally said. "What were you thinking, attacking Porto Belo?"

"It's a rich port," said Captain Tarr. "Our holds are full, and you will do very well out of the raid."

"It was reckless! Porto Belo is Spanish territory. Neither of our countries are at war with Spain at present, and you have stolen one of their women." He gestured to Magdalena and I dropped my knife with a clatter. "You could have started another war with your actions!"

I stared at Sharpe, shocked. *He kidnapped this woman!* The regard I had for him was shattered. Cheval sniggered beside me and I glanced at him. He was enjoying this.

Hornigold waved his hand. "There won't be a war over a single raid and one woman," he said, dismissive.

Erik flushed red, and I flinched before his fist connected with the table. "You don't seem to realize just how precarious your position is, any of you." He glared round the table. "Morgan is suspended and Governor Lynch wants him gone—preferably hanged. And Lynch won't stop with Morgan—he wants total power over Jamaica, he'd see every one of Morgan's men in chains and shipped off to London for trial as pirates. He can't touch me or Vader, but all of *you* are in his sights." He stared at Tarr, who dropped his eyes. Nobody looked at Erik now except Jan.

"My son is quite correct," he said. "Morgan is finished, and you do not have many friends in these waters at the moment. You took an unnecessary risk and have given Lynch all he needs to arrest you."

"What do you propose?" asked Tarr, his jaw set as he stared at Erik.

"You keep well away from Jamaica, and from New Spain. Their ships are fair game, but leave no witnesses. Bring the ships and their cargoes here. Any coin you find is your own."

"Now wait a minute." Tarr banged his own fist on the table. "There are valuable cargoes out there, we won't just hand them over! Not many ships carry coin enough to be worth the risks, not when the haul is to be shared with near two hundred men!"

Erik stood and leaned forward, bracing himself with both hands on the table. I pushed my chair back a little.

"You *will* hand them over. In return, you will have safe haven on this island—out of Lynch's grasp. If he attacks here he risks his own war, and London has already suffered enough at the hands of Amsterdam. If he attacks a Dutch island now, it will be him in chains in a cargo hold bound for London, and he knows it. Sayba is your best chance. You work for us now, and we will keep you free."

Tarr and the other pirates glared at him, but said nothing. Erik sat back down and beckoned to Klara, who placed a plate of meat before him, then served everyone else.

We ate in silence.

Chapter 20

The three of us sat in the drawing room, still not speaking, and I picked up the cushion cover I was embroidering for something to do. The pirates had escaped as soon as the meal was over, and I couldn't help but worry about Magdalena. I jumped and exclaimed out loud—I'd pricked my thumb with my needle. The van Eckens glared at me, but didn't ask after my welfare. I sucked my thumb and examined my work for blood. Clean.

She'd seemed wary of Hornigold, and I couldn't blame her, but Sharpe was also attentive and, truth be told, his attentions had at least appeared welcome. I sighed, even if she was in trouble, there was a not a thing I could do to help her.

I pricked my thumb again and put my work away in exasperation. If I carried on, I'd only ruin what I'd already completed.

Klara brought more drinks. I took another glass of wine, then she carried brandy over to Jan and Erik. I gasped to see Erik blatantly fondle Klara's bottom when he took his glass.

Jan leapt to his feet, furious, and shouted in Dutch. He swept his arm across, connected with Klara's face, and she fell.

"Klara!" I rushed to her. She was conscious, but already her eye was closing and that side of her face seemed to be swelling.

Erik also jumped to his feet, and the two men stood a fraction of an inch apart, both bright red, spitting their words in rage.

Klara and I cowered on the floor, wondering what they were saying. I remembered what she'd said about Jan and how he hated her—if I had any doubt of that before, I had none now.

We both flinched as Jan struck again. Erik didn't fall, though. Nor did he raise his hand to his jaw. He stood and stared at his father, then turned and left the room.

Jan glanced at the two of us still huddled on the floor, but said nothing. He was clearly embarrassed. He walked past us, careful not to get too close, and stood in front of his dead wife's portrait. He spoke to it in Dutch, then left the room.

"Are you all right?" I asked Klara.

She nodded and stood. "I'm scared, Miss Gabriella—he really is going to kill me, he hates me so much."

I didn't know what to say. I thought she was right. I'd never seen anyone so angry or full of vitriol. We looked at each other a moment longer, then Klara moved to collect the shards of the glass scattered over the floor.

I looked up at the picture of Adelheid, and started to pity her. *How long will it be before that sour expression lives permanently on my own face?* I turned back to Klara.

"We'll find a way to keep you and Jan safe, Klara. I promise. We'll find a way."

She looked at me and smiled; I think in pity. She didn't look reassured.

Part 3

7th October 1683

Chapter 21

"Help, help, the molasses!"

We all looked up at the scrawny, filthy boy who had run into the dining room. It took me a moment to recognize him as Klara's boy—he was covered in a thick sticky brown substance.

"What's the meaning of this?" Jan thundered, slamming his open hand against the table top. "Get that out of here!"

Klara had run to her son as soon as he entered the room and placed herself between him and Jan van Ecken, who stood and glared at the boy.

"The molasses! Flood! The molasses!"

Jan strode over to the boy, pushed Klara out of the way and struck him. The younger Jan fell to the floor, sobbing in terror.

"Talk sense, boy, what's happened to the molasses?"

"Tank broke! Molasses everywhere!"

Jan took in a sharp breath and kicked the boy. Klara and I screamed, but the six-year-old only managed a grunt.

Jan Senior looked at Klara cradling her son, and drew his leg back for another kick.

"Vader!" Erik warned, and stepped in front of his father, a restraining hand on his chest. Things had calmed down since their fight, but I held my breath, wondering what was going to happen now.

Jan glared at his son a moment, then nodded. I sighed in relief. Erik knelt down by little Jan and said, "Now, boy, tell us what happened."

I looked at him in surprise at the tender note in his voice and glanced at Klara, but all her attention was on her son.

"What happened, Jan? Tell Mama what happened."

The child sobbed and curled tighter in Klara's arms, she bent her head to his murmur, then looked up. "One of the molasses' tanks has burst. It's flooded the road, just as the men were walking back. They need help!"

"But those tanks were full," Erik said. "They were to be shipped next week." He looked at his father. "We've lost a fortune!"

"Those men could be losing their lives," I snapped at them. "Come on!"

They rushed out of the room, followed by Hans and Hendrik, who had heard the commotion from the cookhouse.

"Come on, Klara, maybe we can help, too."

"Wilbert?"

Jan looked at her.

"Jan, is Wilbert safe?"

"I don't know, Mama. They were all covered, I couldn't see who was who."

"Come on, Klara, we'll go and see—go and help Wilbert."

She nodded and got to her feet. She was in shock, and I grabbed her arm and pulled to get her moving faster.

"Are you well, Jan, can you walk?" I asked him. He winced as he got to his feet and coughed, but nodded. I smiled at him, impressed by his bravery, and hated the van Eckens a little more for the way they treated this child.

We left the room and followed Jan's sticky footprints back out of the house and down the road to the sugar mill.

Chapter 22

Klara and I reached the junction and stopped in shock. A thick river of brown syrup blocked the way. Brisingamen was cut off—no carriage would get through that. Even the air seemed impassable—sickly sweet and cloying; it seemed to stick in my throat as I breathed.

We could hear shouts from up the mill road and looked at each other in dread. Klara was clinging onto Jan, holding him close, and was almost as filthy as he was. I looked at him and shuddered—if he'd been in the way of that river of treacle . . .

Klara moved to the bank and climbed up into the field of sugarcane stumps, dragging Jan after her, and I followed. We cut through to the mill road and stopped. The road was lower than the surrounding fields and had acted as a channel. It was now full of molasses. Molasses-covered men moved at the edges, trying to haul out those caught in the middle.

I jumped when Klara screamed a name: 'Wilbert!"

One of the molasses-covered men turned and rushed over to us, grabbing Jan and holding him tight, then Klara. The three of them hung onto each other and sobbed. Klara was soon only recognizable by her hair.

I looked back at the molasses river, wondering what to do. I couldn't see Erik and Jan anywhere—I doubted they were any of the treacle-covered rescuers I could see. I went closer to the edge. Sticky brown shapes heaved in the mess and showed life. Unmoving humps showed where life had been lost—there were many; too many.

Hans and Hendrik and half a dozen unrecognizable men were in a line, dragging a heaving shape out of the morass into the safety of the sugarcane, and I hurried over as the victim reached higher ground.

I tore a length of cloth from my petticoat and used it to wipe the dense syrup from the man's nose and mouth. I realized the orifices were completely clogged and the man hadn't been able to breathe for some time. I sat back on my heels in despair, then screamed as something struck my chest and I fell to the side, winded.

"What the hell are you doing? Don't touch those filthy animals!" Erik raised his cane to strike again and I cowered in the field, waiting for the blow.

"*Zoon*, Son," Jan cautioned, and Erik lowered his cane then turned and stalked up the hill back to the collection of buildings at the top of the lane.

Jan offered me a hand and helped me up, but said nothing. He escorted me to Erik's side, standing with Rensink, and we looked down at the mess.

"Aren't you going to help them? Somebody may still be alive," I ventured, stunned at my treatment, but even more appalled at the sight before my eyes. As far as I could tell, Jan and Erik had done nothing to help the rescue effort. I coughed in the sweet air.

"What happened?" Erik demanded of Rensink.

"One of the hoops of the full tank snapped," Rensink said. "The men were on their way home and molasses just . . . engulfed them. They didn't have a chance. I was still up here, reprimanding the boy, or I would have drowned too."

"Reprimanding the boy?" Jan asked. "Why, what did he do? Was this his fault?"

"No, no," Rensink said. "I caught him chewing on some

cane—gave him a hiding, but he saved my life."

Jan looked disappointed. I realized Rensink was in shock. I breathed a sigh of relief. Little Jan's sweet tooth had saved him from a horrific fate.

"Get those men organized, Rensink, the ones that are left. Anyone still in there is dead now. I want the molasses collected and re-boiled. We'll have lost a fortune from this, but we'll rescue what we can. It'll make an inferior rum, but at least we'll get more sugar, and it can't be helped. And don't use those tanks anymore—if I remember rightly, they came from Hornigold. It wouldn't surprise me if they were riddled with shipworm!"

I stared at him in disbelief, horrified at their indifference to the deaths of so many men in their care.

Chapter 23

Everything stank of sweetness. Everything was sticky—the very air seemed to be composed of sugar. It had been three days since the accident, and most of the molasses had been shoveled up and put on to boil—the muck of the ground skimmed off as it rose to the surface. The road to Eckerstad was open—although lined with molasses. Six men had lost their lives.

Klara coughed as she brushed my hair; we were all coughing, but the men who'd been caught up in the flood were the worst afflicted.

"How's Jan?" I asked her.

She shook her head. "Not good. He's still struggling to breathe, and the coughing's so violent, I keep thinking it will shake his little body apart."

"Remember what the doctor said—it's just our lungs clearing the residue. We'll all stop coughing soon."

"Mmm," she said. The doctor had only seen Jan, Erik and myself. I'd begged the van Eckens to allow the doctor to see everybody else, especially the children, but they'd refused to spend money on the health of slaves—there were plenty more available if need be. I was hoping the diagnosis he'd given us held true for the others, but I was concerned for little Jan.

"The men are being buried this morning," Klara changed the subject. "At the cemetery on the other side of our village."

I nodded. Jan and Erik hadn't mentioned it to me and were unlikely to attend. Klara knew I'd want to pay my respects to the men who had died, despite my husband and father-in-law's indifference.

After an awkward, silent breakfast, I slipped out of the house and took the northern path away from Eckerstad into the jungle. The sugarcane hadn't reached this side of the estate yet—another thing Jan and Erik argued about: Jan wanted to keep the sugar plantation small and concentrate on shipping; Erik wanted to expand both.

I passed Rensink's house—a modest two-story building—and continued to the slave village. A collection of huts housed the women and families—I knew Klara shared one of them with Wilbert and Jan—and there was also a long, low building where the single men slept.

The village was empty and I paused. I walked up to the men's hut, opened the door and peered inside. The room was lined with wooden platforms and, as my eyes got used to the dim light, I saw a manacle and chain at the foot of each bed. There was no privacy, no comfort, no nothing. I imagined the life these men led—breaking their backs in the fields or sugar mill by day, sleeping like this by night. My fear and dislike of the van Eckens hardened and I realized I'd started to despise them.

I left the men's hut and continued to the cemetery. It was already far too large for such a community, and my tears dripped throughout the service. Rensink led the mourning—another insult—and in Dutch.

Nobody understood what was being said for their lost colleagues, friends, husbands. English-speaking slaves fetched a higher price than Dutch, and by keeping their language private, the van Eckens could talk freely without anybody knowing their business. This funeral meant nothing, and nobody participated bar standing as expected with bowed heads.

"We'll give them a proper send-off later," Klara told me, "in our own way." I nodded. "It would be better if you stayed away, though." I nodded again. I understood that as a van Ecken I wouldn't be welcome.

Chapter 24

I got ready for dinner quickly so that Klara could go to the funeral proper, then went downstairs. Captain Hornigold was sitting with the van Eckens in the drawing room, and I stopped in surprise on seeing him. His company was the last thing I needed, especially as he was on his own and hadn't brought Mr. Sharpe.

I said little at the table, still shocked after the accident. Hornigold was surprised at the extent of our coughing, and I could see he was uncomfortable until Erik explained and he realized the house hadn't been struck down by fever.

The fact that we were all afflicted, however, didn't stop my father-in-law berating Hans and Hendrik for their own difficulty in breathing. I smiled at them, aware they were missing the funeral for their fallen friends. Hendrik tried to return my smile, but broke down in a coughing fit worse than anything I'd heard so far.

"For God's sake, shut up!" Jan shouted. Hendrik did his best, but clamping his mouth shut against the coughs made them worse, and I jumped to my feet as he collapsed. I pulled his hand away from his mouth and was horrified to see a black treacly substance covering his palm.

"Right, that's it, I've enough of this had!" Jan exclaimed. "Cough, cough, cough! And now look, that rug ruined is!"

There was a small spot of coughed-up molasses on it.

"Hornigold, your arrival proves propitious to be. The sugar is waiting to be transported to Cornelius's rum distillery in Sint Eustatius, you can load up *Freyja*, and us as well take. We need to get away from this foul air—the sea air will do us all good and our lungs clear. By the time we return, the slaves will either recovered or died have."

I looked at him in renewed shock at his callousness.

"We can't leave now, Vader, it's our busiest time. We need to oversee the rest of the sugar manufacture and the clearing of more jungle for the next field. We *can't* leave."

"Rensink can that handle, I want us to spend a month or two away from here. This stench and the constant hacking is driving me mad. It will good business be to Onkle Cornelius personally see. It's been too long since we've him a visit paid, I'm sure he thinks he can advantage take. If we deliver the sugar personally, we can a harder bargain drive."

"But Captain Aalbers and *Adelheid* will be putting in soon to take the sugar," Erik protested.

"That's his bad luck. He can *Adelheid* refit for slaves and to Africa head. It will more profits bring, anyway. Gabriella, get that slave of yours to pack, we're in the morning leaving."

"I want Klara and her son to join us," I said. I knew better than to use little Jan's name.

"No," Jan said. "They stay here."

"You told me she was mine to do with as I wished, when I first boarded *Freyja*," I said, my whole body tense with fear at standing up to him, but I knew it could be little Jan's only chance. "I can't manage without her now, not with the way Erik likes me to dress."

I glanced at my husband, gambling that he'd take my side. He had shown small moments of tenderness toward the boy, and still enjoyed Klara's company at times. Plus his relationship with his father was fraught at best. I held my breath.

"I think it's a good idea. My wife needs her slave, and the boy will be useful as well. Klara can't look after the three of us by herself. If you insist on us making this trip, Klara and the boy will join us."

Jan glared at his son, and I let out my held breath– very quietly.

Nothing was said for some time as father and son stared at each other.

"Very well," said Jan, eventually. "Your whore and her bastard son with us come."

I stared after him in shock as he strode out of the room. Erik continued eating and ignored us. I couldn't bear to look at him and watched Hans bundle Hendrik out of the room.

Chapter 25

"Welcome aboard," Sharpe said to me, taking my hand and kissing it. I smiled at him in greeting. He stood a little apart from Hornigold and Cheval, who were greeting my husband and his father. Klara and Jan boarded behind us, and Sharpe nodded to them in greeting. The other men ignored them.

Sharpe led us below, and I made for the cabin I'd used on my first passage.

"No, Magdalena and I have that one. Hornigold has vacated the captain's cabin for the use of you and your husband." He indicated some structures on the deck that hadn't been there last time. "We've erected temporary cabins for him and Mr. van Ecken Senior, although we'll have to take them down again if we get into a fight." He laughed and opened the door to the captain's cabin.

I smiled at him and entered, followed by Klara and Jan, then looked around. I smiled again. It was bigger than the other, and I was relieved. I'd been dreading sharing such a small space with Erik. Whilst the coming days would still not be pleasant, at least there was a little more space to help me endure the journey.

The meal had been awkward and mainly silent; even our coughs had reduced. I hadn't been able to chat with Sharpe or speak to Magdalena, and had no desire to talk to anyone else at the table. Erik was still angry about leaving Brisingamen, and Hornigold and Cheval appeared to be sulking—they must have had other plans than sailing to Sint Eustatius with the van Eckens and a hold full of sugar. The only one in any good humor was Jan, but even he had tired of the atmosphere and lapsed into silence by the time Klara put the main course before us—roasted goat.

The men left us to go on deck and Klara served both myself and Magdalena with wine, then took a tray of brandy and glasses to the men. Magdalena and I were alone.

I looked at her, suddenly nervous. She was a few years older than I, maybe twenty two or twenty three. Her hair curled down her back—way past her shoulders. Her skin was pale and freckle- and blemish-free, and I put my hand to my own freckled face in shame. Her green eyes glittered in the lantern-light over a long straight nose and full mouth. I had no idea how to ask her if she'd been kidnapped or needed help; I couldn't imagine this woman needing anything I could offer. Then she smiled, and her whole demeanor changed. I smiled back and sipped my wine.

"How are you enjoying married life?" she asked in English.

I grimaced. "It's not what I'd hoped," I answered truthfully.

She smiled, though looked sad. "No, I expect it rarely is," she said. We sat in silence for a while.

"I should be married now too," she said, breaking the silence. She stood, walked to the windows and stared out into the night. "To my childhood friend."

I looked at her in expectation, but she did not explain. "What happened?" I asked at last.

Her shoulders tightened, but she didn't turn back to me;

she seemed to be talking to the empty sea. "I loved him, I really did; it's just that . . . he was all I knew."

"What do you mean?"

She didn't answer for a moment, then, "Porto Belo and Panama were all I knew, and I wanted to know more. My fiancé did—he sailed the world trading goods for my father—I hoped to join him on his voyages once we were married, but I knew he wouldn't allow it. He was too traditional, too protective. I would have had a life alone, waiting for him to return, not knowing when or even if he would come back." Now she turned, looked at me, then approached and sat down.

"I wanted adventure," she smiled, "but got a little more than I bargained for."

I looked at her in confusion.

"Leo was overdue from a voyage to Spain, and I was keeping an eye out for his sail. We were to be married once he'd arrived home, and I was both looking forward to seeing him and dreading it. At first, I thought the sail was his, but realized it wasn't when it was joined by a second. I didn't give them another thought until the first cannonball was fired—they were pirates!"

I drew my breath in sharply, even though I already knew who it had been. I was surprised she was opening up to me and wanted to encourage her. I guessed she was as lonely as I was.

"The ships in the harbor sank as they were holed, then the buildings started to fall."

"Did you have no defenses?" I asked, genuinely horrified as I pictured the scene.

"Not then—the treasure fleet calls at Porto Belo twice a year to load up silver from the mines inland and take it to Spain. Before their arrival, and during their stay, the town is heavily fortified, but once they've sailed, there's nothing left to guard. The men either return inland or sail with the fleet, and the town's reduced to an ordinary merchant town again. The forts are barely manned."

I nodded, trying to imagine it: one day busy, rich and important; the next abandoned, ignored and under fire.

"Once the buildings had been destroyed, the pirates came ashore to loot and take whatever they could find. Hornigold found me." She stared at me, but showed no expression.

"Hornigold?" I was surprised. "I thought Sharpe . . ."

She shook her head. "Sharpe was horrified. He's a good man, you know." She looked at me again, eyebrows raised. I offered her a small smile. Admittedly, I thought him the best of a bad lot, but he was still a pirate—I couldn't go as far as agreeing that he was a good man.

"He's Captain Tarr's nephew," Magdalena continued. "And Hornigold is terrified of Tarr. Sharpe makes the most of it. He 'confiscated' me." She laughed. "Hornigold was furious! But he gave me up."

"Had he— Did he . . ." I didn't know how to ask and stopped. She shook her head.

"He didn't hurt me—Sharpe didn't give him the chance, thank the Lord." She looked up, crossed herself, and muttered a short prayer.

"So now you're with Sharpe." I said, surprised at the tone of my voice. I couldn't decide whether it was disapproval or anger.

Magdalena stared at me, cool now. "Yes, now I am with Sharpe."

"Do you miss your fiancé?"

She gave no answer, but her face showed so much pain that she had no need to.

"That's why Hornigold is in such a bad mood," I finally said, embarrassed by the lull in the conversation.

"Yes, he's jealous."

I raised my eyes and looked at her. We sat staring at

each other a moment, then she continued, "That's why we came to Sayba. We were hoping to rendezvous with Captain Tarr. His ship is bigger, and Henry wants to get me away from Hornigold—he does not trust him."

Henry. I'd forgotten his first name. I nodded at her.

"But now we have to endure another passage with Hornigold and his sycophantic crony, Cheval."

I smiled at her description.

"At least you seem to be comfortable," I said, nodding at the cabin next door.

"Oh, yes." She smirked. "We're definitely comfortable." She relaxed her smile. "And it's certainly an adventure."

Chapter 26

Magdalena had left some time ago, and I was almost ready for bed. I sat while Klara brushed my hair, and thought about the woman I'd spent the evening with. I liked her, I thought, though I felt sorry for her family left behind in Porto Belo. They sounded wonderful. *How could she have left them like that to go in search of adventure?* I knew she hadn't left entirely by choice, but it was clear that she'd hoped to join the pirates, and had stayed rather than run from them. *And what of her fiancé, Leo? What became of him?*

I sighed and stood, then crossed to the bed. Whatever her motivations, I was sure she regretted them now. She hadn't bargained on Hornigold; and whilst she seemed happy enough with Sharpe, there had definitely been a wistful note to her voice when she spoke of her childhood sweetheart.

I got under the cover, whispered goodnight to Klara—she would spend the night on a mat on the floor with little Jan—and tried to sleep. I had no idea if Erik would join me, or whether he also had one of the small temporary cabins that had been erected on the gundeck. I prayed I had seen the last of him for the night.

I woke to a cold draught—the bed clothes had been thrown off. Moonlight bathed the cabin and I could see Erik standing over me, swaying with the motion of the ship and removing his clothes. I hoped it was a dream, but knew it was not. My heart sank.

Naked, he climbed in next to me—there wasn't much room, and I was pressed up between him and the cabin wall. Tears started to fall.

He lifted his thumb and wiped my cheek, smiling. I looked at him in surprise at his tenderness, then realized he was enjoying my tears, my fear. I resolved not to give him any more. His hand dropped from my face and pushed my nightshift up. I didn't protest, nor help. He did not care.

He straddled me and I bit my lip to hold in my gasp of pain at his entry. I looked up at him in the moonlight, keeping my face calm and my eyes dry. He looked away. I closed my eyes for a moment at my small triumph, but realized his thrusts had grown more urgent. Then I understood what he was looking at, and opened my eyes again to make sure. Yes, he was staring at Klara, while he was . . . while he was . . . on top of me. I looked at his face, but couldn't read his expression. I didn't recognize it, I'd never seen it on his face.

Then I realized I *had* seen it before—on Hornigold's face when he'd asked for Klara on my passage to Sayba. And on Cheval's face, too. It was desire. I looked at her, huddled on the floor, her back to us, arms around her son to protect him, and felt the tears threaten again.

I turned my face to the wall and stared, refusing to give life to my tears. I felt utterly humiliated. I didn't want to be here, aboard this ship, married to this man, here in this bed.

My mind drifted, and I imagined my little beach, the sand warm, the waves gentle. I imagined walking to the water's edge and sitting on the wet sand, my toes digging into it.

A wave cooled my feet, then pulled at them and the sand around them. I dug my toes in again; again the sand was washed away. It wasn't enough. Suddenly I wanted to be in the water, have it wash me away, rather than the sand. I removed my clothing—it took only an instant—and waded into the sea.

The waves were larger now, crashing into me, jolting my body, over and over and over, one after the other. But I kept going; I would not go back. The rhythmic motion soothed me and I lay in the water, letting it caress and comfort me. I felt bruised and battered, but it didn't matter, the water took the pain away. The sea eased my distress and rocked me as a mother would a babe.

The waves calmed, but still I floated, drifting, drifting, knowing I could return whenever I wanted.

Chapter 27

I stared around me. Nothing. No land; just sea. I closed my eyes, smiled and lifted my face to the sun. But for the noises of the ship and its men, I could be completely alone. I opened my eyes and turned away from the aft rail and the emptiness, back to the ship.

About half the crew were on deck, working the sails or doing other sailor things, and I watched the men up the masts in amazement—they moved so fast, yet so surely they should have been born squirrels.

My eyes searched for my husband—it had become my habit to know his whereabouts so that I could avoid him. There he was, near the mainmast with Sharpe, his father close by at the rail.

I saw a small shape running along deck and grinned— Jan. He never walked when he could run; he was always so full of life and excitement, and was worse aboard ship—he loved it, even following the crew up the knotted ladders of rope that led up the masts. I don't think Klara knew about that though.

A coughing fit hit him mid-stride and he stumbled, crashing into Jan Senior and knocking him back against the rail of the ship. I cried out, my hands to my mouth, shocked. This was just the excuse Jan had been looking for to rid himself of his namesake.

He shouted and grabbed the child, hauling him back to

his feet and toward the rail, still shouting—I couldn't tell whether in English or Dutch—but his intention was obvious: he was going to throw Jan overboard.

Jan's screams froze me to the wooden planking, but they made Erik move. He joined the pair, shouting himself, and grabbed hold of the boy, preventing his father from lifting him any further.

Jan Senior let go and the child fell, then scurried to the mainhatch, his face awash with tears. He jumped below decks and was gone, presumably to find his mother.

Erik and his father were still arguing at the rail, and it looked to be as bad as any argument I'd witnessed so far. Jan prodded his son's chest once, twice, three times, and Erik swatted his hand away. Jan's voice rose even further, his face bright red. Erik's temper rose to match, and he prodded his father in return. Jan didn't hesitate, and swung his fist. Erik took a couple of steps back, but this time he was not going to submit. He had witnesses, and witnesses who were much more important to him than Klara and myself.

He stepped forward and threw his own fist, snapping Jan's head back. Jan tried to step back to regain his balance, but had nowhere to go—he was already against the rail.

His body angled further back until his feet lifted and he tipped over. I hardly heard the splash. I stood rooted to the spot in shock.

I jumped at a hand on my arm: Sharpe. I hadn't noticed him join me at the stern; all my attention had been on the van Eckens. I looked him in the eye and he slowly shook his head. I knew he'd seen what I had seen: as Jan fell, he had held his arms out to his son, who had made no move to catch him.

I looked back at Erik, now leaning over the rail shouting,

"*Vader, Vader!*" and shivered. He had just killed his own father.

"Man overboard!" Sharpe shouted beside me. "Heave-to! Man overboard!"

The ship turned, and the sails shook, then roared. Men pulled one of the towed boats alongside and set off to look for Jan.

An hour later, they returned. Nothing.

"The weight of his frockcoat will have pulled him under," Sharpe said to me. "He wouldn't have had a chance—he's gone."

I nodded, but said nothing, just stared at my husband who was still playing the part of distraught son. Nobody had approached him—even Hornigold watched from a safe distance. *Do they all know it had been no accident?*

I made my way to the mainhatch, wanting to get away from the maindeck and the sight of my husband. I dreaded him seeing me and demanding I play the part of the mourning daughter-in-law. I had to find Klara first, and tell her that she and her son were safe.

Chapter 28

I stared into the mirror and smiled at Klara as she dressed my hair. I had never seen her so relaxed; her eyes sparkled and an easy smile sat on her face. I remembered how surly she'd been when we first met—it was good to see such a change in her.

We'd arrived back at Brisingamen yesterday and I'd barely seen Erik. He'd spent the rest of the journey to Sint Eustatius locked in his father's small cabin—all I'd heard of him was the occasional call for more rum.

When we anchored in Oranjestad Bay he appeared: eyes dull, skin pale, but clean and shaven; and went ashore to greet his uncle. I'd been left aboard the ship. Apparently he'd told his uncle of his brother's death, claimed we didn't have the proper mourning attire, and I would remain secluded until we could put back out to sea.

The sugar was unloaded, Erik finalized the details of the sale, and *Freyja* loaded up with fresh food and water. We set sail again in less than a week. I hadn't been allowed out of the cabin, but was not upset to have avoided meeting more van Eckens.

The return journey had been uneventful—Erik had remained in his father's cabin and I'd spent the majority of the passage with Magdalena and occasionally Sharpe. I'd enjoyed their company, despite the difference in ages.

After our arrival home the day before, Erik had

sequestered himself in the study and I'd eaten alone. I was enjoying the new routine, but tonight the usual Freyjamen were dining with us and we would have Erik's company. I hoped Sharpe would bring Magdalena.

I was surprised when Erik took Jan's seat at the head of the table, although was not sure why—he was the head of the household now, after all. It just seemed disrespectful—too soon.

I was directed to Erik's old seat at the foot of the table and was pleased. I may have to sit facing him, but he was a long way away and I would not have to talk to him.

Hornigold and Cheval sat to my left, Sharpe and Magdalena to my right. I focused my attention on them.

The starter course passed without incident—soup flavored with pumpkin and peppers. Then Hendrik brought in the main—spiced and roasted boar—and the level of noise in the room rose from a respectful and mournful quiet to excited anticipation. Klara poured more drinks and I sipped my wine, feeling suddenly anxious.

Cheval leaned closer to me as the meat was carved. "I know it's a terrible time, but you look very good in black, Madame, you should wear it more often." I blinked and stared at him in surprise, then glanced at Erik. He looked angry.

"Thank you, Cheval," I said and took another sip of wine, then glanced at Sharpe on my other side and widened my eyes in disbelief. He smirked and Cheval thumped his glass down hard enough to break the stem.

"Ah, pardon, pardon!" he exclaimed with a nervous look at Erik. He waved the apology away with a grimace and Klara cleared up the mess, then brought and filled another glass. The table lapsed into uncomfortable silence and it was a relief when everyone had been served and we could eat.

I glanced at Sharpe again and grimaced. He smiled back.

"So, Hornigold, now my father has gone we have a little more freedom."

I looked at him in shock.

"You are aware he and I did not always see eye to eye, especially where your role in our business was concerned. You will find I am more . . . accommodating to your ideas."

The table silenced.

"Erik, please, we're still in mourning," I protested without thinking. I jumped when he immediately slammed his fist onto the table top.

"I was not talking to you, wife! Be good enough to keep your silence until I do."

I glanced at Magdalena and Sharpe in embarrassment, but their eyes stayed on their plates.

"Look at me when I'm talking!" He thumped the table again and I looked at him.

"There will be many changes around here now that I'm master of Brisingamen and governor of Sayba." He glared around the table, and it was clear that he really meant now that he was master of us. My embarrassment turned to fear.

"Hornigold, you will stay here until Captain Tarr arrives, then the three of us will discuss my plans." Hornigold nodded once. "Until then, I wish to reward you for your concern and actions when Vader died. I was pleased with how quickly you reacted to put a boat off to look for him, and how efficient you were at Sint Eustatius."

He glanced around the room and his eyes rested on Klara. She froze.

"Take my wife's slave for the night; she will reward you for me." He laughed.

"Erik, no!" I shouted, horror-stricken.

He stood and thumped the table again. I shrank back in my chair.

"Yes! She is mine to do with as I will—as are you. You will never disagree with me in public again!" Another thump. "Do you understand?"

I glared at him. His threat was obvious.

"Do you understand?" he repeated, his voice low. Sharpe touched my wrist in warning and I nodded.

"Get your hand off my wife, Sharpe. I've been watching you and you're far too friendly. Keep your distance—you already have one whore, let that be enough for you!"

I gasped, and Sharpe stared at Erik, withdrew his hand and nodded. Magdalena's face reflected pure fury, but she wisely kept her silence.

"Klara, you will entertain Captain Hornigold tonight. Take the blue room and do not disappoint him—I do not want to hear any complaints tomorrow."

I risked a glance at her—tears ran down her face. I looked back at Erik; he was smiling. He raised his glass as if for a toast, but said nothing. He looked at each of us in turn, then drank.

Chapter 29

I dressed for bed alone, Klara was already with Hornigold and I shuddered. *Why is Erik doing this to her?* I'd always thought he felt tenderly toward her; it was Jan who had hated her. *Is he trying to make it up to his father? Some kind of twisted apology for letting him die?*

I shuddered again and climbed under the bed sheet. I glanced at the door in trepidation. I hardly dared hope he would leave me alone, but prayed for it anyway.

Tonight, the prayers didn't work—his step was loud on the stairs to my room. He stumbled through the door and I watched his progress in the gloom. He was drunk—he'd thrown glass after glass of wine down his throat after pronouncing Klara's sentence, then called for brandy.

He used the pisspot, threw his clothing to the floor and muddled his way through the thin tester curtains. He grinned at me, enjoying my fear.

"You're mine, wife, and so is that whore. I can and will do with both of you as I wish. Do not anger me, or I will give you to worse than Hornigold." I stared at him, too revolted to react. I believed him.

He straddled me and pushed up my shift. As usual, I neither helped nor hindered. He was right: I was his, and completely powerless.

He tried to push inside me and I bit my lip in anticipation of pain, but there was none. I looked at him in surprise—there was nothing there.

His eyes met mine and he slapped me. "Teef—bitch," he said. He hit me again, and now I could start to feel something down there. He grabbed a fistful of my hair and yanked my head back. I cried out in pain and was aware my throat was exposed and vulnerable. He recognized my fear and grew bigger.

He bent his mouth to my throat and I bit my lip, terrified at what he would do. He kissed my skin, gently, and laughed at my cry of surprise. I'd expected a bite and he knew it. He was playing with me.

Tears ran down my face and I stifled a sob. I tried to push him away, but my efforts had no effect.

"Stop it," he said, pulling my hair again, and I did, scared he would snap my neck.

I remembered that night aboard *Freyja* with him and shut my eyes. I could not take my body away from this, but my mind didn't have to stay.

I pictured my beach. It was gloomy, with storm clouds overhead and rain poured down.

Something smashed into my face. "Open your eyes!" I saw my husband's face, red with anger, but I didn't react. I stared past him, at the canopy, and returned to the beach.

My nightgown was already saturated from the rain and I ran straight into the sea, the surf battering me. I was knocked down, the wave spinning the world about me, but I found my feet and pressed on. The next wave hit me and I staggered back and lost my footing, but this time managed to stay on the surface. I swam forward, deeper and deeper, the storm surge buffeting my body.

Lightning lit the sea around me and I realized I could no longer see the shore. I didn't care. I was safe out here in the waves. I was not safe on land.

I rode the next wave, and the next, then a particularly large one broke early—it felt like stone hitting me, not water. I spluttered my way back to the surface and looked for the next one. It wasn't there.

The waves rocked me now, rather than threatened. The sun was coming out, the sea calming. The storm was abating.

I rolled onto my back and floated on the surface, allowing the sea to rock me to sleep. I knew I wouldn't drown, not now. I was alone here. I was safe. I had survived.

Chapter 30

I woke on sand. I blinked my eyes open slowly—the sunlight hurt them and they felt wrong. I looked around and smiled, relieved. I was on my beach. I'd been washed up on my beach. I was safe. I sat up and cried out in pain. My whole body hurt. It had been quite a storm and the waves had taken their toll on me.

I blinked my eyes open. Weak dawn light showed me the familiar white canopy over my bed. I clenched my fist and lifted it to within my sightline. It held fabric, not sand. I frowned in confusion, then remembered the night before. I was not on my beach; that had been a dream. I was in my bed—my marital bed.

I gathered my courage and turned my head to the side. Erik wasn't there; he was gone. I breathed a sigh of relief which ended in a sob. He wasn't here to enjoy my distress so I surrendered to it, scarcely able to breathe through the violence of my tears.

When they were finally spent, I jumped and cried out in surprise. Klara stood there with a breakfast tray. We stared at each other, taking in the other's bruises, shamefully aware of our own.

"I didn't think you would want to go to the dining room this morning," she said and placed the tray on the bed.

I shook my head, or tried to, relieved and thankful, but not yet trusting myself to speak.

I pushed myself up to a sitting position—very carefully—and winced as I leant back against the headboard. Klara glanced at me in concern, but I ignored her and looked at the tray.

Fruit—pawpaw and carambola—both ripe, both easy to eat. Bread (untoasted) and preserves: the usual jar of mammee apple that I enjoyed, and another, larger jar, that I did not recognize.

I picked up the cup and sipped tea. It was definitely more palatable with three teaspoons of sugar. I put the cup down and ate some pawpaw. Perfect—soft enough that I didn't have to chew; tasty enough to stimulate my appetite; its juice mild enough not to sting the cut on my lip.

I lifted the lid of the strange jar and looked at Klara. I recognized the smell; it was full of the salve we used to ease the bruises left by my stays. Tears started to fall again, and Klara sat on the bed and put her arm around my shoulders. I leaned against her.

"We're going to need a lot of this stuff," I said through my tears.

"I know. I've told Belinda, she has an army of slaves out in the jungle picking what she needs whenever they have a chance." She squeezed my shoulder, but neither of us managed to laugh.

I pulled myself together and sat up. I looked at her.

"What are we going to do?"

She shrugged. "I don't know. He may just be mourning his father. He may return to being the Erik he was before Mijnheer Jan died."

"Klara, the Erik he was before Jan died, killed his father! This *is* Erik. This is the *real* Erik. God knows what he's capable of without Jan here to temper him."

Tears rolled down her face and she sobbed. "What are we going to do? What are we going to do?"

I held her. "I don't know, Klara, I don't know."

I stared at the wall. We were trapped here, with a monster. We had to find a way out—if we didn't find a way, and find it soon, he would kill us both long before our times. I thought back to my beach—pictured the sand and the waves. I had to find a way to the sea. We'd be safe there. Life had changed again; this time I would find a way to escape my fate.

* * * * *

Gabriella's story continues in *Dead Reckoning*, please see Karen's website for more details:
www.karenperkinsauthor.com/valkyrie

For more information on the full range of Karen Perkins' fiction, including links for the main retailer sites and details of her current writing projects, please go to Karen's website:
www.karenperkinsauthor.com/

If you would like to contact Karen and/or join Karen's mailing list to be kept updated with news, upcoming releases and special offers, please go to:
www.karenperkinsauthor.com/contact

Acknowledgements

Many thanks to everyone who has helped me with their time and editorial skills, in particular Louise Burke, Peter Mutanda and all those who gave me the benefit of their time and advice on www.authonomy.com. A big thank you to Cecelia Morgan for designing a wonderful cover – and to Connie Turner for lending me her eye!

Thank you to my family and friends for all their encouragement, as well as everybody in the writing group – the first people to read the book – for all their comments and support.

About the Author

Karen Perkins is the international award-winning and bestselling author of six fiction titles in the Valkyrie Series of Caribbean pirate adventures and the Yorkshire Ghost Stories. All of her fiction has appeared at the top of bestseller lists on both sides of the Atlantic with over 200,000 downloads so far.

Her first Yorkshire Ghosts novel – *The Haunting of Thores-Cross* – is a silver medal winner for European Fiction in the 2015 Independent Publisher Book Awards, and *Dead Reckoning: A Caribbean Pirate Adventure* reached the top 50 in the UK Kindle chart as part of *The Hot Box* set that also included work by international bestselling thriller authors David Leadbeater, John Paul Davis and Steven Bannister.

See more about Karen Perkins, including contact details, on her website:
www.karenperkinsauthor.com

Karen is on Social Media:

Facebook:
www.facebook.com/Yorkshireghosts
www.facebook.com/ValkyrieSeries

Twitter:
@LionheartG

Books by Karen Perkins

<u>Yorkshire Ghost Stories</u>

Knight of Betrayal
The Haunting of Thores-Cross

To find out more about the full range of books in the Yorkshire Ghost Series, including upcoming titles, please visit:
www.karenperkinsauthor.com/yorkshire-ghosts

<u>Valkyrie Series</u>

Look Sharpe!
Ill Wind
Dead Reckoning

To find out more about the full range of books in the Valkyrie Series, including upcoming titles, please visit:
www.karenperkinsauthor.com/valkyrie